A Certain Magical Index

KAZUMA KAMACHI

ILLUSTRATION BY
KIYOTAKA HAIMURA

"… I'm hungry."
Mysterious Girl in White, Index

"Whoa, whoa…!"
Academy City High School Student **Touma Kamijou**

"… Oh, it's the *biri biri* middle schooler again."

"It's your fault, because you're annoying!"
Academy City Tokiwadai Middle School Student Mikoto Misaka

"…Do you want to save Index?!"

"Why do you insist on this futile—!"
Sorcerer Stiyl Magnus
"What?! How can she even use magic...?!"
Sorcerer Kaori Kanzaki

contents

"Is that okay?"

Touma Kamijou's Homeroom Teacher, **Komoe Tsukuyomi**

VOLUME 1

KAZUMA KAMACHI

ILLUSTRATION BY: KIYOTAKA HAIMURA

NEW YORK

A CERTAIN MAGICAL INDEX, Volume 1
KAZUMA KAMACHI

Translation by Andrew Prowse and Yoshito Hinton

Edited by ASCII MEDIA WORKS
First published in Japan in 2004 by KADOKAWA CORPORATION, Tokyo.
English translation rights arranged with KADOKAWA CORPORATION, Tokyo, through Tuttle-Mori Agency, Inc., Tokyo.

Yen On
Hachette Book Group
1290 Avenue of the Americas, New York, NY 10104

www.HachetteBookGroup.com
www.YenPress.com

Yen On is an imprint of Hachette Book Group, Inc.
The Yen On name and logo are trademarks of Hachette Book Group, Inc.

First Yen On Edition: November 2014

Library of Congress Cataloging-in-Publication Data

Kamachi, Kazuma.
[To aru majyutsu no kinsho mokuroku. English]
A certain magical index / Kazuma Kamachi ; illustrated by Kiyotaka Haimura. — First Yen Press edition.
volumes cm
"Translation by Andrew Prowse and Yoshito Hinton"—Title page verso.
"First published in 2004 by KADOKAWA CORPORATION, Tokyo."
ISBN 978-0-316-33912-4 (paperback)
[1. Magic—Fiction. 2. Ability—Fiction. 3. Nuns—Fiction. 4. Japan—Fiction. 5. Science fiction.] I. Haimura, Kiyotaka, 1973– illustrator. II. Prowse, Andrew, translator. III. Hinton, Yoshito, translator. IV. Title.
PZ.1.K36Cer 2014
[Fic]—dc23

2014031047

10 9 8 7 6 5 4 3 2 1

RRD-C

Printed in the United States of America

PROLOGUE

The Tale of the Boy Who Could Kill Illusions
The_Imagine-Breaker.

"... Argh! Jeez, crap! You've gotta be kidding me! Why do I have such rotten luck?!"

Though his scream sounded freakish even to himself, Touma Kamijou continued his incredible escape.

Dashing through a back alley in the middle of the night, he quickly threw a glance over his shoulder.

Eight.

Despite having run more than nearly two kilometers already, there were *still* eight of them. Touma Kamijou, being neither a cook from some foreign legion nor a cyber ninja who'd survived to modern times, had no chance of winning against so many of them—even three was just way too many to handle in a high schooler's fight. It didn't matter how strong you were. It was just impossible.

Kicking a grimy bucket, Kamijou kept running as if he were chasing off black cats.

July 19th.

Yeah, it's all July 19th's fault. It's the day's fault that I hit an unusual emotional high, shouting, "Hooray, tomorrow's summer vacation!" It's the day's fault I went to a bookstore and bought a manga that obviously wasn't going to be good, then went into a restaurant when I wasn't even hungry, thinking, Why don't I splurge! *where I saw a girl who looked like she was in middle school getting harassed by a thug who was clearly drunk, and although something like that would never occur to me, I thoughtlessly decided to help out*... Kamijou's deviant train of thought was running away from him.

He hadn't considered that all the punk's friends would suddenly come out of the restroom.

I always thought going to the bathroom in groups was reserved for girls. Yeah.

"...I ended up having to dash out of there before I even got to see my Hell Lasagna topped with goya and escargot, and now I'm getting treated like I skipped out on the check. I didn't even eat! Man, what did I do to deserve all this rotten luck?!"

Scratching his head frantically, he broke out of the alleyway and onto a main street.

Moonlight had descended on Academy City. Even though the city itself took up a third of the Tokyo metropolitan area, he saw nothing but couples on dates wherever he looked. *It's because it's July 19th; it's all this date's fault!* Kamijou, who was single, screamed internally. Everywhere around him, three-bladed wind turbines sparkled in the illumination of the moon and the city's lights like an aristocratic bachelor's teardrops.

Kamijou sliced through the night, tearing couples apart.

He glanced down at his right hand as he ran. The power inside it was useless in this situation. It wouldn't help him take down a single thug, it wouldn't raise his test scores, and it wouldn't make him popular with girls.

"Ugh! Just such rotten luck!!"

If he did manage to shake his relentless delinquents brigade, they could always call up reinforcements on their cell phones or bust out motorcycles to chase him down or something. So he was trying to run them all ragged until they dropped. To do that, he needed to dangle himself in front of them like bait in hopes of making them tire themselves out. It was basically a boxer's rope-a-dope strategy, letting an opponent punch himself out until his stamina was drained.

Most importantly, though, he wanted to help.

There was no need for this to turn physical. All he had to do was wear them down until they gave up. That would be victory.

Kamijou had some confidence in his ability to run long distances. His pursuers, on the other hand, had already ruined their bodies with alcohol and cigarettes, and the boots they were wearing weren't made for sprinting. They'd find themselves unable to go much farther if they kept running full speed without trying to pace themselves.

He weaved through main streets and alleys alternately, making himself look like a dork fleeing for his life. He watched as the thugs dropped out one by one, falling to the ground on their hands and knees. *It's a perfect solution, and nobody needs to get hurt*, he thought to himself. But what he said aloud was:

"D-damn it... Why do I have to waste my youth on something stupid like this?!"

He was frustrated. Seeing all those couples filled with happiness and sweet dreams around him, Kamijou felt like a loser at life. Summer vacation began the next day. It was pretty depressing not to have any sort of romantic comedy in his life.

Behind him, one of the delinquents jeered, "Stop!! Is running away all you can do, you little brat?!"

These weren't exactly the sort of sweet nothings he'd had in mind, and it rankled Kamijou.

"Shut up! You should be thanking me for not beating the snot out of you, you stupid ape!" he shouted back, realizing he was wasting precious energy in doing so.

...Seriously, you should *be thanking me for not getting hurt, damn it!*

After that, he ran for another two sweat- and tear-filled kilometers. He exited the city proper and came to a large river spanned by a metal bridge that stretched approximately 150 meters long. There were no cars to be seen. The sturdy iron bridge wasn't even lit up, just blanketed by an eerie darkness reminiscent of the sea at night.

As he shot across the bridge, he checked his tail.

He stopped. At some point, he'd thrown off all his pursuers.

"C-crap... Did I finally lose them?"

Desperately fighting the urge to plop himself down right then and there, Kamijou looked up at the night sky and inhaled.

Wow, I really did solve the problem without punching anyone. I think that deserves a pat on the back.

"Man, what the heck was that? Are you pretending to be a good guy by sticking up for those chumps? What are you, some kind of overzealous teacher?"

Kamijou froze.

He hadn't spotted her sooner—there wasn't a single light source on this bridge—but a lone girl was standing about five meters ahead of him in the direction from which he'd come. She wore a gray pleated skirt, a short-sleeved blouse, and a summer sweater. She had every bit the appearance of a completely normal middle schooler.

Staring into the night sky, Kamijou seriously considered just falling backward onto the ground.

It's the girl who was getting hassled at the restaurant.

"...So is that it? Does this mean those guys stopped following me because..."

"Yeah. They were being a pain, so I fried 'em."

He heard the sound of electricity and saw a pale blue flare.

No, the girl wasn't holding a Taser. Every time her shoulder-length brown hair shifted, it buzzed with sparks, as if it were some kind of electrode.

An empty plastic shopping bag fluttered along on the wind, passing in front of her face. Immediately, the bluish-white sparks eradicated it. It was akin to some sort of automatic interference system.

"Whoa." Kamijou grunted tiredly.

Today was July 19th. That was why he went into a bookstore and bought a comic book that was obviously crap, why he went into a restaurant when he wasn't even hungry, and why he'd recklessly opted to jump in when he saw a middle school girl getting harassed by clearly wasted thugs.

However, Kamijou hadn't been thinking, *I should rescue that girl.*

His only thought had been saving the boys who'd crossed her path.

He sighed. The girl was always like this. He'd been seeing her around for almost a month now, but neither knew the other's name. In other words, they weren't striking up a friendship.

She was the one always coming up to him all haughty, saying she'd reduce him to a heap of trash, and Kamijou's job was to shrug it off. There were no exceptions; he stood undefeated.

She'd probably cheer up if he could make it look like she'd won, but he was a pretty bad actor. He tried faking it once before and had subsequently spent the rest of his night getting chased around by what could only be described as a monster.

"...Wait, what did I do again?"

"I will not allow a stronger human than me to exist. That's enough of a reason."

That was all she said.

Even characters in fighting games these days have better fleshed-out setups than her, Kamijou thought.

"I've had enough of you making me look like an idiot. I'm a Level Five esper, got it? Do you think I'd really use my full strength against an incompetent Level Zero? I know plenty of good ways to cook weaklings, you know."

This city, unlike others, didn't follow the traditional scenario where street thugs were the toughest. Those delinquents earlier had been complete nothings—they were Level Zero espers, Impotents, who'd dropped out of the Curricula designed to "develop" their superhuman abilities. The truly strong in this city were people like her: honor student–level espers.

"Um, about that. I already know you have a 320,857th of talent, but you should quit talking down to people if you want to live a long, healthy life, all right?"

"Shuddup. Those guys stoop to gross stuff like injecting drugs directly into their veins and physically shoving electrodes onto their brains, and they still can't bend a spoon. If they're not completely talentless, then what are they?"

"..."

Yes. *This* is the kind of place Academy City is.

Academy City's other face was somewhere that Brain Development—using more palatable names like Mnemonics or Memorization Techniques—was quietly included in the student Curricula.

However, it wasn't like every single one of the 2.3 million "students" in the city **quit being human, like the hero of a comic book**. If you looked at the city's population as a whole, a little less than 60 percent were only at a level where they could bend a spoon if they strained their minds to the point where the blood vessels in their brains exploded. They were all just useless Level Zeroes.

"If you want to bend a spoon, you can just use pliers. And if you want fire, you can just go buy a lighter for a hundred yen. We don't need telepathy; we have cell phones. Superpowers aren't all that special."

This was coming from Kamijou, who carried the stigma of having been labeled a "useless" esper by the Sensors during a citywide physical examination.

"They're all wrong in the head. You're just bragging about some **by-products called supernatural powers**. Wasn't the entire goal to **try and go beyond that**?"

The girl, one of only seven people in Academy City considered to be a Level Five esper, turned her lips down in response.

"Huh?...Right, that. How did it go again? 'Man cannot measure God; therefore, we must first obtain a body beyond that of man, or we can never arrive at God's answers'?"

She snickered.

"It's just ridiculous. What on earth is this 'intellect of God,' anyway? Hey, have you heard? They're developing some military-grade little 'sisters' for me, based on my DNA, that they can use in the army. I guess the by-products were sweeter than the ultimate goal, huh?"

She stopped, her spiel ending abruptly.

The air changed silently.

"...Well. That's what strong people *would* say, isn't it?"

"Huh?"

"Strong people, strong people, strong people. They don't understand how much of a struggle it is to try and accomplish anything because they happened to be born with natural talent. What you just said sounded exactly like a line from the hero in some comic book, oblivious and cruel."

Whzz. zz. zz. He heard a freakish whirring emanating from the river beneath the bridge.

There were only seven espers of her caliber in Academy City. How much of their "humanity" had they had to sacrifice to get there...? A dark flame flickered at the end of the girl's words, hinting to him of that fact.

Kamijou rejected that.

He denied it with singular resolve, by never turning back.

By never losing.

"Whoa, whoa, whoa! Just take a look at the annual physical examinations, will you? My level is zero, and yours is five, the highest! Go ask the people walking around over there, and they'll be able to tell you right away which is better!"

Science was used for Academy City's Ability Development. Things like pharmaceutics, neurology, and cerebral physiology. Even without any talent, if you made it through the standard Curriculum, you'd at least be able to bend a spoon with your mind.

However, Touma Kamijou still couldn't do anything.

Academy City's measurement devices had verified a complete *lack* of talent in him.

"Zero, huh?" the girl repeated, turning the words over in her mouth. Her hand dove into her skirt pocket for a moment, only to reemerge holding an arcade token.

"Hey, do you know what a Railgun is?"

"Hm?"

"It's some sort of battleship weapon that fires metal shells using superpowered electromagnets. The principle's the same as a maglev train."

Clink. The girl flicked the token into the air with her thumb.

It whirled through the air before landing back on her thumb.

"...It's apparently something like this..."

Precisely as she spoke...

An orange beam of light lanced right past Kamijou's head soundlessly. It was actually more of a laser beam than a lance. He only realized it had come from the girl's thumb because that's where he saw the tip of the ray of light.

A moment later, a thunderclap sounded as if lightning had struck. The shock wave of air being torn apart inches from his ears threw off his sense of balance. Shakily, wobbly, he glanced behind him.

The moment the orange beam collided with the bridge's pavement, the asphalt had been blown inward the same way water is when an airplane crash-lands on the ocean's surface. Having spent its destructive energy in that straight thirty-meter line, it faded into an afterglow, searing its image into the air.

"Even a coin like this has massive power if it's flying at three times the speed of sound. Although it does melt after about fifty meters because of air friction."

Iron and concrete swayed violently as if the structure were an unreliable suspension bridge. The metal bolts holding it together clinked and clanked and shot out of their moorings all over its scaffolding.

"......!!"

Kamijou felt a chill, as if someone had thrown dry ice in his blood vessels.

He thought for a moment that the effect would boil all the moisture out of his body. "Y-you...Don't tell me you used *that* to get rid of those guys!"

"Don't be stupid! I don't use this on just anyone. I don't plan on turning into a homicidal maniac, you know," she answered, her brown hair scattering sparks.

"For those powerless Level Zeroes... *This* was more than enough to get rid of them!"

Suddenly, a pale blue spark flew from the girl's bangs like a horn...

...and a spear of lightning blasted straight at him.

There's no way I can dodge that. It was a bolt of electricity fired from a Level Five esper's hair. It was the same as trying to elude a light-speed lightning strike unleashed from a dark cloud—but only once you saw it coming.

Thoom!! The sound of the explosion hit him a moment later.

He'd immediately covered his face with his right hand. When the electric spear collided with it, the blast not only violently dispersed through Kamijou's body, but it scattered in all directions, blanketing the bridge's steel framework in sparks.

...At least, that's how it looked.

"So, tell me. Why the heck don't you have a scratch on you?"

Her words sounded nonchalant, but she was glaring at Kamijou, baring her teeth in frustration.

The high-voltage current that had splayed around him was strong enough to burn through the bridge's steel frame. But even though it had struck his right hand directly, it hadn't blown the appendage off the rest of his body... there wasn't so much as a singe.

Kamijou's right hand had dispelled the few hundred million volts of the girl's electric attack.

"Jeez, what is that power supposed to even *be*? It's not in Academy City's data banks, that's for sure. If I'm 1/320,857th of a *natural*, then you're probably the city's only 1/2,300,000th of a natural *disaster*," muttered the girl resentfully. He couldn't respond. "If you go around looking for fights with that *anomaly*, then I'm gonna have to crank up the voltage a bit."

"... Yeah, says the one who always loses."

Her reply came in the form of another "Lightning Spear," approaching him at Mach speed.

But once again, the moment it struck his right hand, the current discharged in every direction as if it were nothing more impactful than a water balloon.

This was Kamijou's Imagine Breaker, the death of illusions.

It was the laughingstock of daytime television—but in this city, supernatural abilities had been derived by mathematical formula. If anyone employed such "abnormal power," even if they took the form of divine miracles, he could cancel the abilities without a trace.

As long as it was this abnormal power, even this girl's supernatural ability, her Railgun, was no different.

However, Touma Kamijou's Imagine Breaker could only be used against "abnormal powers" like these. Simply put, it could block an esper's fireball, but it wouldn't block the concrete shrapnel the assault pulverized in the process. In addition, the effect only extended from his right wrist to his fingertips. If the fireball hit him anywhere else, he'd be drowning in flames, so...

I thought...I thought I was...I thought I was really dead! Ahh!

He mustered up his calmest, most composed demeanor. Even if his right hand could completely nullify a Lightning Spear traveling at the speed of light, the fact that it had actually struck his right hand *in the first place* was nothing but a total coincidence.

His heart beat furiously in his chest. He had to summon every shred of his strength to compose a mature grin.

"Man, so unfortunate...such rotten luck, huh?"

With a single sentence of lament to the world, he brought an end to this day, July 19th.

"You really *are* unlucky."

CHAPTER 1

The Magician Stands atop the Tower

FAIR,_Occasionally_GIRL.

1

If you're an Aquarius, born between January 20th and February 18th, you will have extremely good fortune in love, money, and business! No matter how improbable the circumstances, only good things are headed your way! Go buy a lottery ticket! Just don't get carried away with your newfound popularity with the opposite sex—no two- or three-timing, now. ♪

"Man... I knew this would happen... I knew it, but still..."

It was July 20th, the first day of summer vacation.

Touma Kamijou was at a loss for words. His dorm room in Academy City was sweltering because his air conditioner was broken. Lightning had apparently struck in the middle of the night and blown out 80 percent of his appliances. That included his refrigerator, the food in which was now all spoiled. When he went to open his emergency rations—a cup of yakisoba—he accidentally dumped all the noodles down the sink. Then, having no alternative but to go out to eat, he stepped on his credit card while searching for his wallet, crushing it. After that, he decided to sulk back into bed and cry himself to sleep, only to be awakened by his ringing phone. It was his homeroom teacher conveying a heartfelt message: "Good morning,

Kamijou! You're dumb, so you need to come and take your makeup classes. ♪"

The horoscopes on TV were being broadcast like a weather report. He'd known they'd sound like this, but they were so far off it wasn't even funny.

"...I know this is how it is. I've always known, but I can't process it unless I say it out loud..."

Fortune-telling was always wrong, and good luck charms were no better. This was Touma Kamijou's life. Luck had long since turned its back on him. You'd think it would be genetic, but his father had won the fourth place in the lottery (about 100,000 yen) once, while his mother had scored free drinks from the vending machine jackpot multiple times. It was enough to make him wonder if they were even related by blood. But as he wasn't harboring a crush on his little sister and wasn't in line for royal succession, no good would've come of discovering that he wasn't his parents' son.

It just boiled down to the fact that he had bad luck.

Like, so bad it was almost a joke.

But he wasn't going to sulk about it forever.

Touma Kamijou didn't rely on luck, and that enhanced his ability to act.

"...All right, then. The main problems right now are my card and the refrigerator."

Scratching his head quizzically, he looked around his room. As long as he had his bankbook, it wouldn't be difficult to get a new card. The bigger problem was his refrigerator—in particular, his breakfast. For his summer Ability Development makeup classes, he'd need to take medicine like Metoserin pills or Elbrase for sure, so he definitely didn't want to go in there on an empty stomach.

He figured he'd stop by the convenience store on his way to school. He pulled off the T-shirt in which he'd been sleeping and changed into his summer outfit. As stupid students are prone to doing, Kamijou had for no good reason gotten all excited about summer vacation finally arriving, stayed up really late, and now his head throbbed with sleep deprivation. *Making up for four months' worth of cut classes in a single week is a pretty sweet deal, though*, he thought with forced optimism.

Cheering himself up, he declared, "And it's so nice outside that maybe I'll air out the futon today."

He opened the screen door that led to the balcony. When he got back from his class later, his bedding would be all fresh and cozy.

From his balcony, he could see the side of the neighboring building a mere two meters away. "The sky's so blue, and yet I can't see the light!"

A sudden depression washed over him. He'd said it in a bright, jocular tone, but doing so had the complete opposite effect on his mood.

Tortured by the isolation that left him without a straight man, Kamijou hoisted the futon off his bed. He wouldn't be able to die in peace if his futon wasn't at least soft. Bringing down his foot, he felt a disquieting *squish* as he stepped in something spongy. Investigating the cause, he found a piece of yakisoba bread in its clear wrapper. It had been shoved into the back of the aforementioned annihilated refrigerator, so it was probably already sour.

"... Hope we don't have any summer showers today."

What was sadly most likely a premonition spilled out of his mouth. He turned again to the open screen door that opened onto his balcony, only to discover that a white futon was already draped over the railing, airing out.

"?"

Even though these were student dorms, they were basically set up the same way as studio apartments, so Kamijou lived by himself. That being the case, there was nobody but him to go hanging futons from his terrace.

It was only upon closer examination that he realized it wasn't a futon at all.

Hanging over the ledge was a girl wearing white clothes.

* * *

"Huh?!"

His mattress fell to the floor with a *thump*.

The scene was baffling; it made no sense. Some girl was dangling from his balcony as if slung over a metal clothesline, limp and exhausted. Her body was doubled over the rail at her hips so that her arms and legs all drooped, suspended straight down.

She was...fourteen, maybe fifteen? She looked a year or two younger than Kamijou and appeared to be a foreigner, given her fair complexion and white hair. No, not white. Silver...probably? Either way, it was long and obstructed her inverted face from his sight. It most likely reached to her waist.

As for her clothing...

"Whoa. It's a real-life sister...but not the sibling kind."

A habit? You know, the kind of things nuns and sisters in churches wear. Her clothing looked to be all one piece and went down to her feet. A hat perched on her head—or rather, a hood made of a single piece of cloth. In direct contrast to the standard black pigmentation one usually saw with habits, the one the girl wore was pure white. He guessed the fabric was silk. Moreover, points on it were embroidered in gold. Despite the fact that the basic design was typical of a nun's habit, the unusual color completely changed its impression. She looked like some kind of gaudy teacup.

Suddenly, the girl's delicate fingers twitched.

Her head began rising unsteadily from its drooping orientation. Her long, flowing hair smoothly parted to either side to reveal her face, as if a curtain were being opened.

Whoa, whoa...!

The little lady had a relatively cute face. Kamijou, who had exactly zero experience overseas, saw a freshness in her pale skin and green eyes. All things being equal, she looked rather like a doll.

But that's not what had him flustered.

First and foremost, she was a foreigner. He'd once had an English teacher advise him to steer well clear of the wider world for the rest of his life. If somebody from God knows where ever started babbling at him, he'd just buy a down comforter or some other random thing to extract himself from the situation.

"Ai..."

The girl's pretty—though slightly dry—lips parted slowly.

Kamijou retreated one step, and then another. At which point, his foot revisited the yakisoba bread still on his floor with another *squish*.

"I'm hungry."

"..."

In that moment, Kamijou imagined that his feeble brain had substituted the unfamiliar language she was speaking with Japanese, like when dumb elementary schoolers make up silly lyrics to foreign songs.

"Hungry."

"..."

"I'm hungry."

"......"

"Didn't you hear me? I said I'm hungry."

The silver-haired girl slightly impatiently addressed the calcified Kamijou.

This is no good. Clearly this is very not good. This... This just sounds like Japanese.

"Err, umm..." He stared at the girl hanging out to dry on his balcony and inquired, "So, uhh... Are you about to say you just happened to collapse here on your way somewhere?"

"You could say I collapsed here and am dying."

"..." The girl was perfectly fluent in Japanese.

"I'd be very happy if you gave me some food to fill me up."

Kamijou looked down at the prepackaged yakisoba bread, still under his foot and making squishy noises. It looked spoiled.

I don't know what the hell is going on, but it's definitely better not to get involved. I'll let this kid be happy somewhere far away from here, he thought, taking the plastic-wrapped, sour yakisoba bread and thrusting it into the girl's mouth. *Once she smells how rotten it is, she has to run away. In Kyoto, giving someone rice with hot tea is like telling them to go home,* he thought.

"Thank you, I should like that."

She chomped down on the entire thing, wrapper and all. Also her benefactor's hand.

And just like that, Kamijou's day once again began with a shriek and a stroke of bad luck.

2

"First, I should introduce myself."

". . . Uhh, *first*, why were you even hanging there—?"

"My name? It's Index."

"That's a fake name no matter *how* you look at it! You're an 'index'? Like from the back of a book?!"

"As you can see, I'm a member of the Church. That's important. Oh, not the one in the Vatican, but the Puritans of England."

"I have no idea what any of that means, and are you ignoring my question?!"

"Hmm, I'm talking about Index . . . Oh, if you want my magic name, it's Dedicatus545."

"Hello? Heeelloooo? What kind of alien is speaking on this frequency?" Kamijou had no patience left for listening to this girl and picked at his ear with his pinkie finger. She started gnawing on her thumbnail. Maybe a nervous habit?

Why exactly are we sitting politely around my glass table like this is some kind of job interview?

He needed to leave for school soon, or he'd be late for his summer makeup classes. But he obviously couldn't just leave this lunatic in his room by herself. The worst part of it was that this mysterious silver-haired girl calling herself Index looked like she'd taken such a liking to the place that she was rolling around on the floor.

Was this yet another expression of Kamijou's misfortune? If so, this had gone too far.

"Also, I would be very grateful if you filled up this 'index' with food."

"Why?! Why bother raising your parameters?! If I tripped some strange flag and ended up going straight into the Index route, then just kill me now!"

"Umm…is that slang? I'm sorry. I don't think I understand what you mean."

She was a foreigner, of course. She didn't seem to understand Japan's geek culture.

"If I take three steps out that door, I'll die of malnourishment."

"…Um, and I care about that why…?"

"When that happens, I'll be sure to scrawl a message next to my corpse with my last bit of strength. A sketch of your face."

"What…?!"

"If someone actually comes to my aid before I've expired, I might tell them I was held captive in this room and abused until all that was left was this husk of a person…and I'll tell them you forced me to cosplay in this outfit, too."

"You might say *what*?! You seem to know a lot about otaku culture over here after all, don't you?!"

"?"

She tilted her head as if she were a kitten seeing herself in a mirror for the first time.

How mortifying. She's playing dumb. I feel like I'm the only one who's been tainted.

Kamijou stomped into the kitchen. *I'll do it! Okay, I'll do it!* The contents of the refrigerator had been ruined anyway, leaving only garbage. *Even if I let her eat this stuff, it's not like it's putting a dent in my wallet. It'll be fine if I heat it up.* He plopped the remains of what had once been food into a frying pan and started cooking something like a stir-fry.

Now that I think of it, where exactly did she come from?

There were foreigners living in Academy City, too, of course. But

she didn't have that particular "scent" residents had. However, it would be very odd if she was an outsider.

Academy City was known as a "city of hundreds of schools," but it was easier to think of it more like a "city-sized boarding school." It sprawled across a third of Tokyo, but a Great Wall of China–like partition surrounded the whole thing at the moment. It wasn't as strict as a prison, but it wasn't somewhere you could just accidentally wander into and get lost.

At least, that was how it looked to the outside world. In point of fact, engineering universities had launched three satellites into space for research purposes, and they constantly had their shining, watchful eyes on the city. Anyone leaving or entering was comprehensively scanned. Anyone arousing suspicion who didn't match up with the Gate's records would activate Anti-Skills or members of Judgment from all the schools, either of which would be all over them in seconds. Although...

Yesterday, electro girl conjured up a bunch of storm clouds. Maybe that's how she managed to evade their "eyes," Kamijou thought.

"Umm, so why were you hanging out to dry on my balcony, then?"

Kamijou tried again, splashing soy sauce into the malicious vegetable stir-fry.

"I wasn't hanging out to dry, okay?"

"Then what happened? Did the wind blow you here or something?"

"...Maybe something like that."

He'd only been joking. He stopped moving the frying pan and turned back to the girl.

"I fell. I was actually trying to jump from rooftop to rooftop."

Rooftop? he thought, looking up at the ceiling.

This neighborhood was chock-full of cheap student dorms. Slender, identical eight-story buildings were lined up one next to the other. As one could see from the view from the balcony, there were only about two meters between each building. It would probably be possible to jump from one rooftop to the next with a good running start, but...

"But the buildings are eight stories tall. One wrong step and you'd fall straight to hell."

"Yeah. You know what they say—they don't put up headstones for suicides," Index declared. Kamijou didn't really know what she meant by that. "I didn't have any choice, though. There was nowhere else for me to run at the time."

"To... run?"

Kamijou frowned unwittingly while Index replied simply, "Yup."

"I was being chased."

"..."

His hand stopped rocking the hot pan.

"I was actually jumping between buildings just fine, but in the middle of one leap, I got shot in the back." The Index girl looked like she was laughing.

"Sorry. It looks like I got caught on your railing while I was falling."

There was no embarrassment or sarcasm in her voice at all. She smiled at him as if it were perfectly normal.

"You got shot...?"

"Yes? Oh, don't worry, I'm not hurt. These clothes also have a defensive barrier on them."

What's a "defensive barrier"? A bulletproof vest?

The girl spun around to show off her clothes. She certainly didn't look like she was wounded. *Was she actually shot?* He found it much more probable that everything she had said was just a pile of lies, half-truths, and delusions.

However...

At the very least, she really *had been* hanging on his seventh-story balcony.

Hypothetically, if everything this girl was saying was true...

Then who would have shot her?

Kamijou contemplated.

He considered how much resolve it would take to vault across the rooftops of eight-story buildings. How a balcony on the seventh floor had fortunately interrupted her descent. What had she meant by her claim that she'd "collapsed"?

"I was being chased," she said.

He considered the smile plastered on her face when she'd said that.

He didn't know what kind of circumstances Index was caught up in, and he didn't understand much of what she was saying. Even if she'd explained everything to him from start to finish, he probably wouldn't have understood half of it. He also probably wouldn't have wanted to *bother* understanding half of it.

But one thing was true.

She'd been dangling on his balcony on the seventh floor. If she'd taken one wrong step, she could have slammed into the pavement instead. The deadly reality of that fact struck Kamijou so vividly that he felt his chest tighten.

"Food."

Index suddenly poked her face out from behind him. *She can speak Japanese, but... she doesn't know how to use chopsticks?* She was clutching the utensils in her fist like a spoon, her gaze fixed excitedly on the contents of the skillet.

A comparison of her expression to that of a kitten just lifted out of a cardboard box in the rain wouldn't have been far from the mark.

"..Uhh."

Something like a (toxic) vegetable stir-fry comprised of compost simmered in the frying pan.

Hmm. Looking at the hungry girl before his eyes, he could feel Angel Kamijou (normally paired with Devil Kamijou) writhing in agony inside him.

"Uhh, ahh! B-but, you know, if you're that hungry, rather than this gross bachelor chow I threw together, we should do it right and go to a restaurant or order takeout or something!"

"I can't wait that long, okay?"

"...Uhh, ugh!"

"And besides, it doesn't look gross at all. You cooked it for me without expecting anything in return. It can't possibly be bad, okay?"

This time she smiled even more widely and more brightly, in a manner befitting an actual nun.

Kamijou's stomach felt like it was being wrung out like a mop. Index ignored him, taking the chopsticks in her fist and scooping the contents of the pan into her mouth.

Munch munch.

"See? It's not bad at all."

Chew chew.

"...Ah, is that so."

"I can taste that you gave it a bit of a sour tang to help revitalize me. Well done."

"Egck! Sour?!"

Gobble gobble.

"Yeah. But I'm fine with sour. Thanks. You know, you're kind of like a big brother."

She grinned. She'd been eating so ravenously that she had a bean sprout stuck to her cheek.

"...Uhh...Whoooooaaaaaahhh!"

Vwapp!! He snatched the frying pan out of her hands at supersonic speed, and Index's expression became the very picture of disappointment. Kamijou made himself a vow. *I will be the only one to go to hell for this.*

"Were you hungry, too?"

"...Huh?"

"If you're not, then I think you shouldn't play games and just let me eat it."

Index chomped at the tips of her chopsticks and watched him with upturned eyes. Kamijou had a revelation.

God spoke to him: "You must take responsibility and eat this."

His rotten luck hadn't been the problem this time. He'd brought this entirely on himself.

3

Touma Kamijou smiled, his mouth filled with stir-fried garbage.

The girl munched on a biscuit, looking dissatisfied. Holding the biscuit two-handed and gnawing away, she reminded him of a squirrel.

"... So, you said you're being chased. Who's after you?"

Having returned to his senses in the wake of his holy visitation, Kamijou put this question forward as the primary matter at hand.

He'd only met her thirty minutes ago and certainly had no intention of diving to the depths of hell with her. But it probably wasn't possible to forget the whole thing.

So, in the end, I'm just a hypocrite. A fraud. I just want to say I did something to ease my conscience, but there's no way I can help resolve this.

"Yeah...," she responded somewhat drily. "I wonder? Maybe Rozenkreuz or Stella Matitina... I think it's an organization like that, but I don't know its name, since they're not the kind of people who place much value in names."

" 'They'?"

Kamijou treaded carefully. This meant some kind of group was chasing her.

"Yeah," Index answered calmly, despite her situation.

"A sorcerers' society."

....

"I see. Magic, huh...? Umm. What the hell?! You're insane!"

"Ah, er, what? Umm, was that not the correct term in Japanese? Sorcery, like, magic. A magic cabal."

"..." The word *cabal* confused him even more. "What? Is that some sort of hip new cult that forces you to believe in its founder, or else 'thou shalt be divinely punished'? And uses LSD to brainwash you? That would be dangerous in more ways than one..."

"... You're kind of making fun of me, aren't you?"

"Uhh."

"... You're kind of making fun of me, aren't you?"

"... I'm sorry. I can't. I can't do this whole 'magic' business. I know about all sorts of abnormal abilities, like pyrokinesis and clairvoyance, but I can't handle this 'magic' thing."

"...?" Index tilted her little head confusedly.

She probably assumed that someone who believed in the omnipotent power of science would have just rejected what she said outright, claiming that there was nothing unexplainable in this world.

However, a supernatural power resided in Kamijou's right hand.

It was called the Imagine Breaker, and no matter what nonsensical, preternatural force he was up against, his Imagine Breaker could dispel it. It could even negate miracles.

"Supernatural abilities aren't uncommon here in Academy City. Anyone can open 'circuits' and 'develop' by injecting Esperin into your brain, sticking electrodes on your head, and playing some rhythms in headphones. If every facet of something can be explained scientifically, then obviously everyone will accept it as fact, right?"

"... I don't really get it."

"It's obvious! Very obvious, so obvious! Obvious times three!"

"... Well then, what about magic? Magic is obvious, too, right?"

Index grew petulant, as if someone had just told her that her pet cat was stupid.

"Umm... okay, for example, you know janken, right? Wait, was that game played in the rest of the world?"

"... I think it's called rock-paper-scissors where I come from, but I know it."

"Okay, then say I played janken and lost ten times in a row. Would you think there's a reason for it?"

"... Mgh."

"There isn't, though, is there? But it's human nature to start thinking that there *is* something behind it," explained Kamijou, bored. "You start thinking that there's no way you could lose ten times in a row and that there must be some kind of hidden rules working against you. What do you think would happen to those people if you threw some astrology into the mix?"

"...Like, if you're a Cancer, then you're unlucky, so you should stay away from competition?"

"Exactly. Around here, that's what 'occult' really means. The moment we start thinking that hidden forces like 'luck' or 'fortune' really exist, our minds mistake simple coincidences for predetermination. It's illusory."

Index displayed a momentary, almost feline annoyance before saying:

"...So you're not just rejecting what I said without thinking about it first."

"Nope. I can't do this whole worn-out fairy-tale thing specifically *because* I've thought about it seriously. I don't believe in wizards like the ones from picture books. Nobody would develop their brains if you could just use some MP and raise someone from the dead. Even I couldn't believe in any of that occult stuff. It has nothing to do with reality or science."

Supernatural abilities only appear to be "mysterious" because human brains are stupid.

It was common sense that they could be explained away by science here.

"...But magic is real."

Index made her declaration, the corners of her mouth lowering in dismay. This statement was likely the pillar of her convictions, not unlike Kamijou's Imagine Breaker.

"Well, whatever. But why are those people chasing y—"

"Magic is real."

"..."

"Magic is real!"

Looks like she wants me to admit it no matter what.

"B-but what the heck *is* magic? Can you shoot fireballs from your hands? Can you do it without going through an esper's Curriculum? If you can, then why don't you show me? Then I might be able to believe you."

"I don't have any magic power, so I can't use it."

"..."

It's like she's one of those useless espers who claim they can't bend spoons when cameras are rolling because it distracts them.

But it was true that his feelings on the matter were complicated.

Even though he'd said that the occult was implausible and that magic couldn't exist, the fact was that he knew almost nothing about the Imagine Breaker in his right hand. How did it work? What kind of principles did it operate under? Not even Academy City's System Scan, the world's most cutting-edge program of supernatural ability development, could see through his Imagine Breaker. That's why he carried the stigma of an Impotent, a Level Zero.

It was a power he had possessed since birth, not one he'd obtained through a scientific Curriculum.

He claimed that mysticism was unrealistic, but he himself wielded something of the "occult" that defied the rules of reality.

Still, he couldn't just tell himself something nonsensical like, "Well, there are plenty of mysterious things in the world, so it wouldn't be weird if magic *did* exist!"

"...Magic is real."

Kamijou sighed.

"Okay. *If* magic does exist..."

"*If?*"

"*If* it exists," Kamijou continued, ignoring her, "why are people chasing you around? Does it have something to do with those clothes or something?"

He was referring, of course, to her overly extravagant habit, sewn of white silk and gold embroidery. He meant to inquire if it was somehow "religiously motivated."

"...Because I'm Index, the archive of forbidden books."

"Huh?"

"I carry 103,000 grimoires. Those people probably want them."

....

"This conversation just stopped making sense *again*."

"Hey, how come whenever I explain something, all of your verve just *vanishes*? Do you have a short attention span?"

"Umm, I'm trying to organize my thoughts, but I don't really understand what a grimoire is. It's a book, right? Like a dictionary?"

"Yep. *The Book of Eibon*, the *Lesser Key of Solomon*, *Nameless*, *Cultes des Goules*, the *Book of the Dead*... Those are some famous ones. *The Necronomicon* is really famous too, so there's a lot of forgeries and imitations of it, I think."

"Okay, what's in the book doesn't matter."

Swallowing his urge to just call them chicken scratch, he asked:

"So, these 103,000 books... where are they?"

He would absolutely not budge on this one. A hundred thousand books were enough to take up an entire library.

"Does this mean you have a key to a warehouse somewhere or something?"

"No." Index shook her head back and forth. "I have all 103,000 right here with me, and not one less, okay?"

Huh? He frowned. "Can stupid people just not see them or something?"

"Even if you weren't stupid, you wouldn't be able to see them. What would be the point if you could just look at them whenever you wanted?"

Index's words hung in the air between them. Kamijou started to get the feeling she was teasing him. He took a look around, but there wasn't a single moldy grimoire or anything—just his gaming magazines and manga, and his crumpled summer homework sitting in the corner of the room.

"... Ack!" He'd been listening patiently until now. But he just couldn't take any more, and his words caught in his throat.

This whole "being chased by someone" might be a delusion, he thought. *But if that is the case, then she was hopping between eight-story buildings for no good reason. And then she messed up and ended up splayed over my balcony... I wouldn't be able to keep up with someone like her.*

"... It's really weird that you believe in supernatural abilities but not magic." Index scowled again, irked. "Are supernatural abilities really that amazing? Having some kind of special power doesn't make it okay to treat people like dirt, you know."

...

"Well, you got me there." He sighed to himself. "That's right. You're right. It's wrong to think that having a funny trick gives you the right to lord yourself over other people."

His gaze fell to his right hand.

It could produce neither flame nor electricity. It couldn't shine, or make loud noises, or evoke strange patterns on his wrist.

However, his right hand could nullify any and all abnormal powers—regardless of whether the power in question was good or evil, and even if it was a divine miracle like from the legends.

"For the people who live here, having an ability is part of their personality; it's their moral support. So it'd be nice if you could just overlook that part. In the end, I guess I'm one of those people, too."

"That's right, stupid. Hmph. Even if you didn't mess with the inside of your head, you could just bend spoons with your hands."

"..."

"Hmph. What's so great about some *artificial* man who abandoned the *natural world*? Hmph."

"Would you mind if I taped that mouth of yours shut and your pride along with it?"

"I-I will not bow to intimidation!" Index glowered at him like an irritated cat. "B-besides, you keep saying supernatural powers, but what exactly can *you* do, mister?"

"... Err, well, I can..."

He hesitated for a moment.

Opportunities to explain his Imagine Breaker didn't come along very often. And the fact that it only reacted to "abnormal powers" necessitated an understanding of "abnormal" and "supernatural" powers first.

"Well, you see, my right hand... Oh, by the way, I didn't get this through drugs; I'm a *natural* from birth."

"Uh-huh."

"If something touches my hand... If it's an abnormal power, even if it's like a nuclear blast, or a tactical Railgun, or even a miracle, it gets canceled out."

"Huh?"

"... Wait, what's with that reaction? You look like someone showed you a rock that got passed off as a good luck charm on TV."

"Well, I mean, I was just told that *someone* could dispel miracles even though that *someone* doesn't even know God's name."

Surprisingly, Index smirked at him and stuck her pinkie finger in her ear.

"... Ugh. H-how annoying. I can't believe how annoying it is to be mocked by some fake magical girl who claims magic is real but can't even show me any."

He'd been muttering to himself, but his grumbling instantly set her off:

"I-I'm not a fake! Magic really does exist!"

"Then show me something, you Halloween reject! I'll jam my right hand into it, and then you'll believe my Imagine Breaker is real! How's that, Fantasia?"

"Fine, I'll show you!" Index raised her hands, smoke seemingly about to pour from her ears, and cried, "This! My outfit! This is the strongest holy shield you could get, the Walking Church!" Index emphasized her teacup-like habit with outstretched arms.

"What the hell is a Walking Church?! You're making no sense! Quit throwing around gibberish like *holy shield* and *index of forbidden books*, you inconsiderate jerk! Do you even know what the word *explain* means? You're supposed to break it down for people who don't get it. Don't you even understand that?!"

"Wha—?! Says the person who isn't even *trying* to understand!" Index waved her arms furiously. "I'll show you some proof! Go get a knife out of the kitchen and try stabbing me in the stomach!"

"All right, why don't I?!... Wait, you're trying to entrap me, aren't you?!"

"Oh, so you don't believe me!" Index's shoulders were bobbing up and down in time with her ragged breathing. "This is a church in the form of clothing, with all the essential elements of a church crammed inside. The weaving of the fabric, the stitching, the decorative embroidery... All of it was calculated! A simple knife won't hurt me a bit, okay?"

"It won't hurt you... Hey, on what planet would some idiot just say, 'Sure, I'll stab you'? That would be a remarkably new twist on juvenile delinquency."

"I've had enough of you making fun of me... This fabric is a perfect copy of the Shroud of Turin, worn by the saint who was pierced by the Lance of Longinus, so its strength is Papal class, okay? In your words... yeah, I guess it would be like a fallout shelter. It can repel any attack, physical or magical, and parry or completely absorb it... Before, I said I was shot in the back, fell, and got caught on your balcony, right? If I hadn't been wearing the Walking Church, I'd have a bullet hole in me. Don't you even understand *that*?"

Shut up, moron.

Kamijou, his affection gauge toward Index quickly decreasing, regarded her through narrowed eyes.

"... Huh. So, in other words, if your little skirt really is some kind of abnormal power, then it should get blown to smithereens if I just touch it with my right hand, right?"

"*If* your power is actually real! Ha-ha-ha-ha!"

Fine, then! Kamijou reached forward and grabbed Index's shoulder firmly.

It actually felt as if he were grabbing a cloud. The texture was weird, like a soft sponge was absorbing the pressure.

"Wait... huh?"

Now that he'd calmed down a bit, he played through the scenario.

If hypothetically... if what Index was saying was all true—though he still thought it was impossible—then what would happen if her Walking Church had actually been constructed employing some preternatural means?

If his hand erased all aberrant forces, wouldn't her clothes be destroyed?

"Whaaaaaaaaaaaaaaaaaaaaaaaaaaaa—" Kamijou shrieked automatically in anticipation of the completely unintentional and M-rated situation into which he'd been maneuvered.

…

…

…?

"—aaaaaaat, wait…huh?"

Nothing was happening. Nothing at all.

What the hell, man? Don't scare me like that! he thought, though in fact he did feel on some level slightly disappointed.

"See, look! Imagine Breaker? That's nothing! See, nothing happened, did it?"

She beamed at him triumphantly, placed her hands on her hips, and puffed out her chest.

The next instant, like an unbound ribbon on a gift box, all of Index's clothes fell off.

The threads woven into her habit severed cleanly, and the outfit collapsed into a simple piece of fabric.

One piece, however, remained. The hood resting atop her head seemed to be isolated from the rest of the ensemble. It stayed where it was, looking awfully lonely.

Still grinning with pride, her hands on her hips and her chest puffed out, Index froze.

To put it simply, she was stark-naked.

4

This girl named Index apparently had a habit of biting people when she got angry.

"Ow...you bit me all over the place. What are you, the mosquito at summer camp?"

"..."

No answer.

Index, naked as the day she was born with only a blanket to hide her shame, sat on the floor on her knees. She was busily sticking safety pins into the fabric of her habit in a (futile) effort to somehow return her clothes to a wearable state.

An aura of doom dominated the room.

It's not like somebody from the *JoJo* manga had shown up and used his Stand.

"...Uh, princess?"

Kamijou tried again to rouse her, wondering as to the nature of her actual personality.

"...What?"

"I was one hundred percent at fault here, right?"

His alarm clock flew at him in reply, eliciting a yelp. His pillow followed directly after, and then a steady stream of his game systems and cassettes. He couldn't believe what he was seeing.

"You're just going to casually chat with me after that?!"

"Ah no, I'm not! I was bewildered, too, and, uhh, how youthful of us!"

"Stop making fun of me...Grrrrrr!!"

"I underst— Okay, okay, I apologize! That video is a rental, so stop biting it like it's some kind of handkerchief, stupid!"

He comedically put his head down on the ground.

Deep down, though, seeing a naked girl for the first time made his heart feel like it would be squeezed to death.

Touma Kamijou, however, didn't let it show on his face because he was an adult.

...That's what he thought, anyway, but if Touma Kamijou had looked in a mirror, he'd have been pretty surprised at what he saw.

"I'm done," Index muttered with a sniffle. She spread out her pure white habit. She had returned it to some semblance of normalcy through her sweatshop effort.

Dozens of safety pins gleamed brightly on the salvaged habit.

"... *sweat*"

"Umm, are you going to wear it?"

"... *silent*"

"Are you going to wear that iron maiden?"

"... *sob*"

"In Japanese, we call that a 'bed of needles.'"

"...Urgh, grrr!!"

"I get it!" He buried his head in the floor and apologized unreservedly. Index's expression was that of a bullied child, and she was currently gnawing through his television's power cable like a naughty cat.

"I'll wear it! I'm a nun, after all!" With a cry that he didn't really understand, she curled herself up underneath the blanket and started squirming around like a caterpillar to put it on. The only thing visible outside the blanket was her face, which was so red it looked as if it might explode.

"...Huh. Somehow, this reminds me of my swimming lessons."

"...Why are you watching? I think you should at least turn away."

"Oh, whatever. It's no big deal. Unlike before, you changing isn't sexy at all."

".."

Index's motions ground to a halt, but when Kamijou didn't appear to notice, she gave up and squirmed around some more, dressing herself. Her hood toppled to the floor, but she didn't notice; maybe she was concentrating too hard.

It was kind of like being in an elevator, what with the awkward silence.

Kamijou's mind had been steadily drifting away from reality, but the words *summer makeup classes* finally came crashing back to the forefront of his brain.

"Ack! That's right, I have makeup classes!" He looked at the time on his cell phone. "Let's see, umm . . . Hey, I have to go to school now. What are you going to do? If you're staying here, I can give you the key."

The "kick her out" option had already been abandoned.

Since her habit, the Walking Church, had reacted to his Imagine Breaker, there was no doubt that she was somehow involved with abnormal forces. That would mean that not *everything* she said was a lie.

For example—that she had been pursued by sorcerers and had fallen from the roof of a building.

For example—that she was going to continue her life-or-death game of tag after this.

And, for example—that sorcerers straight out of fantasy novels were running around a city where they'd formulated even ESP and PSY.

. . . Despite all that, though, he still felt like he should give the depressed Index some space.

". . . That's okay. I'm leaving."

She leaped to her feet, still ensconced in the doom aura. She passed by Kamijou's side like a ghost. She didn't seem to notice that her hood was still on the floor. If he picked it up carelessly, he'd probably break that, too.

"Ah, uhh . . ."

"Hm? Oh no, you don't get it." Index turned back to look at him. "If I'm here too long, *they'll* probably come this way. You don't want to be blown up with the rest of your room, do you?"

She posed the question unflinchingly, leaving Kamijou at a loss for words.

She sluggishly drifted out through the door that was the entrance to his studio. Kamijou chased after her in a panic. He checked his wallet, thinking maybe he could do *something*. He only had 320 yen left. In spite of that, he energetically burst through the door in an effort to keep Index there. Unfortunately, as he walked out, his pinkie finger slammed at Mach speed into the doorframe.

"Gah, mah! Yaaahh!"

He squealed unintelligibly, bracing his finger against his leg. Index turned back, startled. As he writhed at the intense pain, his cell phone slid out of his pocket. *Ah.* Before he could stop it, it hit the floor, its liquid-crystal display made a *criiiick* noise, and he knew it had suffered a mortal wound.

"Ugh, no . . . ! What rotten luck!"

"It's not rotten luck. I think you're just clumsy." Index giggled. "But if you really do have this Imagine Breaker, then I guess you can't do much about it."

". . . What do you mean?"

"Right. Well, you might not believe any stories of the magical world I come from, but . . ." She smiled at him. "You know things like divine protection or the red thread of fate? If things like that do really exist, then I think your right hand is canceling them out, too."

Index swayed her safety pin–covered habit from side to side and said, "The power in this Walking Church is that of *providence*—divine favor—after all."

"Hang on. Fortune and misfortune just refer to probabilities and statistics. That can't be righ—"

At that exact moment, his finger touched the doorknob and was beset by a brilliant static shock. *What?!* His reflexes kicked in, his body flinched, and his right calf **cramped** in a sudden muscle spasm.

He cried out in silent agony for approximately six hundred seconds.

"..Excuse me, Miss Nun?"

"What is it?"

"..I'd like an explanation."

"Well, it's not much of an explanation," declared Index in a matter-of-fact tone, "but if the story about your right hand is true, then I think just by having it, you're erasing the power of luck altogether?"

"..I see... so you mean..."

"So the very fact that your right hand is touching the air is making you totally unlucky. ♪"

"Gyaaahhh!! What rotten luck!!"

Kamijou didn't actually believe in the occult, but he had a separate stomach when it came to the concept of bad luck. In any case, nothing ever went right for him, fostering a deep impression that the universe bore him a particular ill will.

A lone nun clad in pure white gazed upon him with the benign smile of the Holy Mother herself.

People would say that those were inviting.

"Rotten luck, huh. The fact that you were born with that power in the first place was pretty rotten luck in and of itself, wouldn't you agree? ♪"

Kamijou had started crying at the warmth of her smile without realizing it, but then it finally occurred to him just how far they'd actually strayed from the conversation he'd intended.

"N-no, wait! Where on earth do you plan on going? I don't know what's going on, but if there *are* sorcerers prowling around nearby, then shouldn't you just hide in my room?"

"No, because if I'm here, then the enemy will come here, too."

"How can you know that for sure? If you don't go around drawing attention to yourself and just stay put in my room, then there's no problem, right?"

"But there is, okay?" Index pinched her clothes. "My Walking Church uses magical power. Well, the Church wants me to call it divine power, but it's all the same mana anyway. Anyway, to put it simply, enemies seem to be tracking magical power."

"Then why the hell are you wearing that transmitter?!"

"Because it has absolute defensive capabilities, okay? Though your right hand did smash it to pieces..."

"..."

"To pieces..."

"I'm sorry, okay? I'm sorry, so stop looking at me with tears in your eyes like that! But if my Imagine Breaker broke it, doesn't that mean it isn't transmitting anymore?"

"Even if it didn't, they still would have detected its destruction. Like I said before, the Walking Church's defensive capability is Papal class. It's basically like a fortress. If I were the enemy and I got word that a fortress had been broken, I'd head straight for it in an instant."

"Wait a second. Then that's all the more reason I can't leave you. I still don't believe in the occult, but...how can I leave you when I know someone's after you?"

She gave him a blank, stupefied look.

He really, really could only see the face of a normal girl when he saw that expression.

"...All right, then are you willing to follow me into the depths of hell?"

She smiled sweetly.

That smile was so ripe with pain, it robbed Kamijou of his words.

Index was telling him gently...

...to stay away.

"I'll be okay; I'm not alone. If I can flee to the Church, they'll give me shelter."

"...Hmm. And where is this Church?"

"London."

"That's really far! Just how far do you plan on running?!"

"Huh? Oh, it's all right. I think there is a handful of dioceses in this country."

Seeing Index standing there with her safety pin–speckled habit fluttering in the breeze gave the impression of a battered woman fleeing an abusive husband.

"A church, huh... I think there might be one here in the city."

The word *church* evoked images of the setting for a giant wedding ceremony, but Japan's churches were, frankly, dull. The culture of the cross had never been particularly thick here, and given that it was a nation prone to earthquakes, there weren't a lot of buildings still standing with long histories. The church Kamijou had seen from the window of a train was just a prefabricated house with a cross on top... Though, on the other hand, an ostentatious church seemed wrong, too.

"Hmm. It can't be any old church, though, since I belong to the Church of England."

"???"

"Umm, well, Crossism is one thing, but there are a lot of different kinds." Index smiled wryly. "First, you have Catholicism, the old way, and Protestantism, the new way. And even the old way, which I'm a part of, is split up into Roman Orthodoxism, centered on the Vatican; Russian Catholic, based in Russia; and English Puritanism, with its headquarters at St. George's Cathedral. There's more like that, too."

"...If you went to the wrong church by mistake, what would happen?"

"I'd be turned away," said Index, still wearing a cynical smile. "Russian Catholic and English Puritanism only really exist in their respective countries, after all. English Puritan churches in Japan are rare."

"..." The direction of the conversation was not looking good.

Maybe Index had visited a ton of churches before collapsing out of hunger. If she was turned away at the entrance every time and kept on running, how would that have made her feel?

"It's all right. It'll only be like this until I find a Church of England–style church."

"..."

Kamijou thought for a moment about the power in his right hand, then called after her, "Hey!...If you're ever in trouble, you can feel free to visit again."

That was all he could say.

Despite being the man who could kill even God.

"Okay. If I get hungry, I'll come over again."

Her smile was like a sunflower, and so perfect that Kamijou couldn't say another word.

A cleaning robot passed by Index, diverting from its path to avoid her.

"Huh?!"

Her perfect smile was wiped off her face in an instant. She twitched, then fell over backward, as if her leg had suddenly **cramped**. With a painful-sounding *slam*, the back of her head collided with the wall.

"~~~! Wh-what is this weird thing?!" Index screamed, forgetting about her head.

"Look at the pot calling the kettle black. That's just a cleaning robot."

Kamijou sighed.

Its size and shape were similar to an oil drum. It had small wheels affixed to the bottom, and it spun a circular mop, which looked like an industrial vacuum cleaner, around and around. It also had cameras affixed so it could avoid people and obstacles, but this made it the mortal enemy of miniskirt-wearing girls everywhere.

"...Oh. I heard Japan had unrivaled technology, but you really are living in the age of mechanized Agathions."

"Uhh, hello?" The weirdly impressed Index scared Kamijou. "This *is* Academy City. We've got stuff like this all over the place."

"Academy City?"

"Yeah. Basically, the western districts of Tokyo were developing more slowly than the rest of it, so someone bought up all this land

and built this city. We've got dozens of universities and hundreds of primary schools, all crowded together. It's a city of schools." Kamijou sighed. "An eighth of the city's residents are students, and the buildings that look like apartments are all student dorms."

Though, on its underside, the city necessitated Ability Development for its students.

"That's why the city seems so strange. The automated garbage collection, the wind-powered generators, and that cleaning robot were all originally college lab experiments, and they're all over the city. Our tech level has advanced about twenty years ahead of the rest of the world."

"I see." Index stared intently at the cleaning robot. "So does that mean that all the buildings in this city are affiliated with this Academy City itself?"

"Yeah...I mean, if you're looking for something affiliated with the Church of England, it might be a better idea to leave the city. The churches around here are all probably just places you go to learn about theology and Jungian psychology."

"I see." Index nodded, finally remembering that her head was in extreme pain and cradling it in her hands. "Ow?! Ah, wait? Where did my wimple and veil go?!"

"What, you just realized now? You dropped it earlier."

"Huh?"

What Kamijou meant was, *You dropped it when you were changing inside the blanket*. What Index thought he meant, though, was, *You dropped it when you fell over when the cleaning robot surprised you*. She searched around the floor of the hallway for a few moments, looking confused.

"Ah, I get it! That electric Agathion!"

Having entirely misunderstood him, she dashed off to chase the cleaning robot that had already disappeared around the corner.

"...Hah. She's off."

He looked back at the door. Index's hood was still in there. He looked back down the hallway again, but the girl was no longer in sight. Their parting certainly hadn't been the teary sort.

She seems like the kind of person who'd survive the apocalypse, he thought for some reason.

5

"Okay! Teacher printed some things, so she's going to pass them out first. We'll be using these for this makeup class, okay?"

Kamijou had been in this class for a semester already, but he still thought it was preposterous.

When Komoe Tsukuyomi, the homeroom teacher of Class 1-7, stood behind the podium, all you could see was her head. At 135 centimeters tall, she was famous for being unable to pass roller-coaster safety requirements. No matter how you looked at her, she was a twelve-year-old girl, on whom you'd expect to see a yellow safety hat, a bright red backpack, and a standard-issue soprano recorder. The young female teacher was considered to be one of the school's seven mysteries.

"If you want to talk, then Teacher won't stop you, but you really should listen to what she has to say! Teacher worked hard to make these quizzes, so if you do badly, you'll have to play the see-through game as punishment!"

"Wait, Miss Komoe, are you saying we have to play poker with our eyes closed? That's for the Clairvoyance Curriculum! I, Touma Kamijou, am very worried that we'll end up staying here all night trying to win ten times straight when we can't even see our own hand!"

"Yes, well, Kami doesn't have enough Development credits, so he's going to have to play the see-through game no matter what, right?"

Ack! Kamijou choked. Her smile was all business.

"...Hmg. It seems Komoe thinks Kami is cute as hell."

This was from a blue-haired class representative (a male one) with an earring sitting next to him. Kamijou didn't understand.

"She may look like she's having a good time trying to reach up the blackboard like that, but can't you feel the pure evil flowing from her?"

"...What? If I got a bad grade and she started insultin' me, I wouldn't mind a bit. Hey, your EXP is quite high, having verbal play with a little kid like that!"

"...So you don't just have a Lolita complex—you're a masochist, too?"

"Aha-ha! I don't *only* like little girls, I *also* like little girls!"

Are you an omnivore?! Kamijou almost shouted.

"Hey, over there! If you say another word, you're doing Columbus's egg, okay?"

"Columbus's egg" meant just what it sounded like. He would have to balance an egg upside down on his desk without any support. Even students specializing in psychokinesis had to exert their brains to the brink of exploding to make the egg stay still, since if they used too much psychokinetic power, the egg would break. Difficulty: lunatic. If you didn't succeed, you would end up in detention until morning.

Kamijou and Blue Hair had the wind taken out of them and returned their attention to Komoe Tsukuyomi behind the podium.

"Is that okay?"

The smile on her face was absolutely terrifying.

Even though Miss Komoe liked being called "cute," she despised being called "little."

However, she didn't seem to care much about being looked down upon by the students. It was kind of inevitable in this Academy City. With 80 percent of the entire population being students, it was a veritable neverland. Even compared to normal schools, these "salaryman teachers" were treated harshly. Moreover, a student's strength was based as much on his or her powers as academic ability.

A teacher was someone who "develops" students, and the teachers themselves lacked these talents. The gym teacher and guidance counselor here could blow away even Level Three monster-students with a single fully trained fist. Sort of like a member of the "elite squadron of foreigners," but it would be cruel to expect something like that from Miss Komoe, the chemistry teacher.

"...Yo, Kami."

"What do you want?"

"Did ya get turned on when Miss Komoe told ya off, bro?"

"That was just you, moron! Just shut up, idiot! I haven't awakened any psychokinetic ability, so I don't have time to play with a lowbie. And quit it with that fake Kansai accent already!"

"...D-d-d-don't call it fake! I'm really from Osaka, dude!"

"Shut up, you rice-farming country bumpkin. You're ticking me off. Quit making dumb comments already!"

"W-we don't farm rice! Ah, ah, aah! *Takoyakis* are so good!"

"Stop forcing it! Are you gonna eat rice with *takoyaki* for me? Just for your character?"

"What are you trying to say? Even people from Osaka don't eat *takoyaki* exclusively all the time."

"..."

"They don't, do they? I don't think they do...Er, wait. Maybe... No, no way...But...Huh? Which is it?"

"Your armor is cracking apart, you Kansai wannabe."

Kamijou sighed and looked out the window.

This makeup class is pointless. I should have stayed with Index.

The habit she'd been wearing, the Walking Church, certainly had *reacted* to his right hand (although *reacted* might have been putting it too mildly), but it still didn't make him believe in magic per se. Ten to one, she'd been lying about most of it, and even if she hadn't been lying deliberately, she might have just been confusing the occult for simple, natural phenomena.

But still.

...I let a big one get away, huh?

He let out another sigh. He was just going to be chained to his desk in this classroom, boiling hot for lack of an air conditioner. He should have given that "swords and magic" fantasy a shot instead. It even had a cute heroine thrown in for good measure. (He hesitated to call her pretty.)

"..."

He remembered the hood that Index had left in his room.

In the end, he hadn't returned it. He knew that it wasn't because he *couldn't* return it. Even if he'd lost sight of her, he probably would have been able to find her pretty quickly if he'd tried. And even if he hadn't found her by now, he'd currently be running around the city with her hood in one hand.

When he thought back on it, he felt that maybe he wanted to keep some sort of a connection. That maybe she would one day return to retrieve what she had forgotten.

The girl in white who'd graced him with a perfect smile…

He needed to leave a connection behind.

He was scared of his memory of her disappearing like an illusion.

What the hell?

After mulling it over rather poetically, Kamijou finally figured it out.

He realized that he didn't dislike the girl who'd fallen onto his balcony. He at least liked her enough to regret not having to deal with her again.

"…Ah, damn."

Tsk. Had he known he'd feel this way, he'd have tried to stop her.

Now that I think of it, I wonder what she meant when she said she carried 103,000 grimoires.

Kamijou had been told that the people after Index, the magic cabal or whatever (*does cabal mean it's a corporation?*), were chasing her because they wanted the 103,000 grimoires she possessed and was continuing to run away to protect.

And what she carried wasn't a key to a huge warehouse packed with books or a treasure map or anything.

When Kamijou'd asked where they all were, Index had said, *Right here.* But as far as he could tell, there wasn't a single book on her. Besides, his room wasn't big enough to hold 103,000 books in the first place.

I wonder what that was about?

He considered the situation, tilting his head slightly. Her habit, the

Walking Church, had reacted to his Imagine Breaker, so not *everything* she'd said was a complete delusion, but...

"Hey, Teach? Mr. Kamijou's ogling the girls' tennis team outside and isn't paying attention to your lecture," declared Blue Hair in his forced Kansai accent. Kamijou grunted out a "Huh?" and his train of thought made a U-turn back to the classroom.

"..."

Miss Komoe was silent.

She looked like she was in serious shock to discover that Touma Kamijou wasn't entirely focused on her class. Her expression was akin to that of a twelve-year-old in winter discovering Santa's true identity.

Immediately, the class, defending a little girl's innocence, directed hostility-laden, piercing stares at Kamijou.

Despite the fact that these were only summer makeup classes, Kamijou ended up getting detained until the hour school normally would've dismissed.

"...What rotten luck."

The ill-fortunes boy muttered to himself, staring up at the three-bladed wind turbines glistening in the evening sunlight. Goofing off at night was strictly forbidden, so the buses and trains in Academy City generally aligned their final runs with the end of the school day.

Having missed the last bus, he walked through the glaringly hot streets of the shopping district. A police robot passed by him. It, too, looked like an oil drum with wheels attached; it was essentially a moving security camera. They had originally been upgraded versions of canine companion robots, but since apparently they were drawing too much attention from children to do their jobs effectively, every worker robot in the city was altered to the same basic oil-drum design.

"Oh, there you are. Hey, yo, you! Hang on a min— Hey! You, I'm talking to you! Stop already!"

As Kamijou, fried from the summer heat, gazed at the slow-moving police robot, he didn't initially register that the voice was directed at him. He was busy thinking, *I wonder where Index ended up after she finished chasing around that cleaning robot.*

He finally turned. *What does she want?*

It was a girl who appeared to be in middle school. Her shoulder-length brown hair took on a reddish shine in the evening glow. Her face was painted an even brighter shade of red. She wore a gray pleated skirt, a short-sleeved blouse, and a summer sweater. At last, he placed the face.

"...Oh, it's the *biri biri* middle schooler again," said Kamijou, referring to the sound of the electrical crackling she emitted.

"Don't call me Biri Biri! I have a name, you know: Mikoto Misaka! Remember it already! You've been calling me Biri Biri ever since we first met!"

Since we first met? Kamijou thought back.

Ah, that was right. She'd gotten involved with some delinquents the first time they'd crossed paths, too. At first, he'd just thought some kids were trying to steal her wallet, and he'd decided to help her out. (He'd figured that, in a best-case scenario, his intervention might have earned him a visit to the underwater dragon palace like Urashima Tarou had.) Instead, for some reason, the girl got angry and started shouting, "Get out of here! Quit poking your nose into other people's fights!" *Biri biri!* At which point Kamijou, of course, had blocked her voltaic attack with his right hand, eliciting a confused "...Huh? Hey, how come that didn't work? Then how about this! Whaaat?" The final result of this initial encounter was, of course, their present relationship.

"...Huh? What's this? Mommy, I'm not sad, but tears are coming out."

"Why the heck are you spacing out like that...?"

Still burned out from his makeup class, Kamijou decided to brush off Biri Biri.

"The girl glaring at poor, exhausted Kamijou is the Railgun girl

from yesterday. She seems terribly disappointed at having lost a fight, and ever since, she's been tracking him down day after day, trying to get back at him."

"...Who the heck are you narrating to?"

"She's stubborn and hates to lose, but deep down, she gets lonely easily and is a member of the animal club at her school."

"Stop making up a weird backstory for me!!" shouted Mikoto Misaka, flinging her arms out to the side. Her motion drew the attention of nearby pedestrians. This was understandable; her featureless, bland summer uniform was actually that of Tokiwadai Middle School, one of the five most distinguished schools in Academy City. The elegant and refined young ladies from Tokiwadai could be easily spotted even in rush-hour crowds, so if one of them started acting like a brat, sitting on train floors or fiddling with her cell phone, anyone would have been shocked.

"So, what is it, Biri Biri? Wait, it's July twentieth, summer vacation, right? Why are you wearing your uniform? You got makeup classes?"

"Erk...Sh-shut your mouth."

"Did you come see the cute bunny at the animal shed at your school?"

"I told you to quit it with that strange animal backstory! Anyway, I'm gonna jolt you so hard today that you'll twitch like a frog hooked up to a car battery, so get your last will and testament ready, you jerk!"

"I don't wanna."

"Why not?!"

"Because I'm not a member of the animal club."

"Grr...Why you little...!!"

The middle schooler forcefully stomped down onto a road tile.

In an instant, all of the cell phones in the vicinity gave off an incredible, simultaneous *crackle*. The wired broadcasts in the mall disconnected with a *bzzt*, and the police robots running around cried out with a terrible *fizzle*.

Biri biri. Her hair chirped with static electricity.

The Level Five esper, with the power to generate a Railgun with her body, bared her teeth like a beast and grinned.

"Hmph. How about now? Did that flip a switch in your cowardly brain?...Mmph!"

Kamijou frantically covered her mouth with one hand, covering her entire face in the process. "Sh-shut up!" he whispered angrily. "Please, just close your mouth and be quiet! All the people whose cell phones you just fried are looking for someone to murder right now!! If you give us away, they'll all want to be compensated for the damage! And I don't even want to think about how much all that broadcast equipment costs!!"

He recalled the silver-haired nun for some reason and offered a fervent prayer to the God who he usually only remembered on Christmas.

As if his prayer had been answered, no one came their way.

Thank God, thought Kamijou, still delicately suffocating Mikoto. He sighed in relief.

"...Message. Message. Error number one-zero-zero-two-three-one-Y-F. Electromagnetic field in violation of the Radio Law detected. System abnormality confirmed. To protect yourself against cyberterrorism, please refrain from using any electronic devices."

Imagine Breaker and Railgun turned around in a panic.

The oil-drum drone was rolling around the road, sputtering and venting smoke. It continued its unintelligible babble.

A moment later, the police robot issued a shrill alarm siren that was audible to everyone in the vicinity.

Of course, they ran.

They fled through alleys, overturning a grimy bucket as if shooing away black cats. *Wait a minute. Why am I running? I didn't do anything wrong*, Kamijou thought as he ran.

Oh, that was right. He'd once heard on a variety show that a single police robot costs 1.2 million yen.

"Ugh..." He sobbed. "Wh-what rotten luck...Just because I'm even remotely associated with someone like this."

"What do you mean 'someone like this'?! I have a name, and it's Mikoto Misaka!"

The two of them finally came to a stop in a back-back-back-back alley. It was a square lot, as if one of the buildings in the line had been demolished. It looked like a perfect place for street basketball.

"Shut up, Biri Biri! You were the one who called down the ridiculous lightning yesterday and killed all my electronics! You still got something to say?!"

"It's your fault, because you're annoying!"

"That doesn't even make sense! Besides, I haven't so much as touched you, you idiot!"

After that... Kamijou used his right hand to block every attack Mikoto threw at him. It wasn't just her Railgun. She used a whip sword made of magnetized iron shavings, powerful electromagnetic waves intended to disrupt his internal organs, and she even brought down an actual lightning bolt from the heavens as her finishing move.

But none of them can withstand Touma Kamijou.

No matter what sort of aberrant anomaly she employed, he could completely eradicate it.

"You just wore yourself out from attacking me! You just exhausted yourself by using too much power! Don't blame your lack of stamina on me, Biri Biri!"

Grrr. Mikoto groaned and clenched her teeth as hard as she could. "Don't give me that! It's impossible! I haven't gotten hit at all, so doesn't that make it a draw?!"

"... Okay, jeez, fine. You win, Biri Biri. Beating you up isn't gonna fix my air conditioner, anyway."

"Gah... ! W-wait a second! Take this a little more seriously!!" she shouted back, arms flailing angrily. He sighed.

"So you're saying you want me to get serious?"

Mikoto choked on her words.

Kamijou casually formed a fist with his right hand and repeated his question. The mere gesture made her break out in a heavy, unwelcome sweat. She froze, unable to retreat a step.

The reality was that she didn't have a clue as to the true nature of his power. To her, he was an unknown threat who kept all his trump cards neatly tucked away behind his poker face.

It was only natural for her to get skittish. He'd deflected her every attack for more than two hours now and didn't have a scratch on him. She had to consider: *If he actually got serious here, what would happen to me?*

But he simply sighed and turned away.

The invisible threads binding her body finally loosened. She wobbled one step, then another.

"...This is pretty rotten luck." Kamijou was actually shocked that she'd been shocked. "The appliances in my dorm are all fried, this morning I had to deal with some fake sorcerer, and now this electro-esper..."

"A-a sorcerer? What's that?"

"..." He thought for a moment. "...Hmm, what *is* it, indeed?"

Had Mikoto been her usual self, she would have shot back with: *Are you insane, you moron? I knew your power was freaky, but is your* brain *freaky, too?!* This right before laying into him with another lightning-bolt barrage. Today, though, she was nervous, as if anticipating something. His act had been a bluff to fool his opponent, of course, but it pained him a little to see how effective it really was.

But still, a sorcerer, huh.

Kamijou remembered a little. The word had casually come up several times when he was with the nun in white, but now that he was away from her, it sounded surreal.

He wondered why he hadn't felt this way when Index was around.

Maybe she had something—something mystical, something that made him believe.

"...Wait, what the heck am I thinking?"

Kamijou mumbled, paying no attention to Biri Biri, or Mikoto Misaka, who at the moment bore a striking resemblance to a cowering puppy.

He'd already cut his ties with Index. In this big, wide world, coincidentally encountering someone a second time for no reason was next to impossible. There was no point in wondering about sorcerers.

But he still couldn't forget about her.

She'd left the pure white hood she wore on her head in his room.

That one last connection clawed its way into a hole in his heart, irritating him.

He honestly didn't understand why he felt this way.

Despite being the man who could kill even God.

6

These days, 320 yen couldn't even buy a large serving of beef bowl.

"..Medium..."

Girls that nibble at their tiny bento boxes wouldn't understand, but for growing, sweaty boys, medium-size beef bowls were really just snacks.

After chasing away the spark-plug girl, Mikoto Misaka, he enjoyed his snack at the beef bowl place. With thirty yen (after tax) remaining in his wallet, he walked back to the student dormitory, now covered in shadow.

No one was around.

It was the first day of summer vacation, so everyone was probably out having tons of fun in the city.

At a glance, the building looked like any old studio apartment complex. There was a line of tightly packed doors on the straight path along the wall of the square building, guarded by a portcullis-like metal railing. Since this was a boys-only dormitory, there were no "miniskirt-peeping prevention" plastic sheets on them.

The student dorm buildings stretched away from the road. He could see the building entrances on the sides and the individual balconies lining the gaps between the buildings.

The entrances had automatic locks on them these days, but the distance between adjacent buildings was only two meters. It would be easy to infiltrate another building if you jumped across the roofs as Index had this morning.

He disengaged the lock, slipped past the **closet that they called the administrative office**, and got on the elevator. The elevator had a unique charm to it. It was even more cramped and dirtier than elevators used at construction sites, and the R button indicating the roof was blocked by a small metal plate in order to prevent roof-hopping Romeos.

The elevator made a microwave-like *ding* and stopped on the seventh floor.

The door opened with a groan. Kamijou helped push it aside, then exited onto the walkway. It was seven floors up, but it didn't feel like a very tall building. It seemed needlessly hot and humid, maybe because of the oppressiveness of the building next door.

"Hm?"

It was then that Kamijou noticed. On the other end of the straight path, in front of the door to his own room, were three cleaning robots. Three was an unusual sight. There were only five cleaning robots assigned to this building in the first place. They were each moving back and forth with short, quick motions, so he thought there must be a pretty nasty mess there.

...For some reason, an extreme foreboding of misfortune settled over him.

Those oil-drum droids had enough destructive force to tear off pieces of gum stuck to the ground on main roads. Just what on earth needed three of them to tackle it? He shuddered—maybe it had been his next-door neighbor, Motoharu Tsuchimikado, in another one of his delinquent, drunken tirades aimed at losing his virginity, throwing up all over the floor there instead of on the electricity pole outside the door of his room.

"Just what on earth...?"

People have a rather peculiar compulsion to witness disaster.

Taking another step or two forward, he finally saw the source.

The mysterious girl, Index, had collapsed on the floor from hunger.

* * *

"..Ah"

He couldn't see her whole body behind the robots, but the downward-facing white habit pockmarked with shiny safety pins made it clear she'd collapsed there.

She didn't flinch, even though the three oil-drum robots were ramming her with a rhythmic *clunk-clunk*. The scene had an air of tragedy, as if city crows were pecking at her corpse. But cleaning robots were programmed to avoid humans and other obstacles. Not even robots treated her as if she was human? What was that all about?

"...How should I put it? It's rotten luck." Kamijou muttered something along those lines. Had he checked his expression in a mirror, though, he'd have been surprised. He was actually smiling.

Something inside him had been "stuck" on her. Even if he didn't believe in sorcerers, the situation could have been construed as a suspicious new cult chasing around a lone girl.

The fact that she'd turned up again as if nothing had happened (?) made him happy.

Even setting all that aside, he was just glad they got to meet again for some reason.

Kamijou thought back to the one thing she had forgotten—the pure white hood he hadn't returned to her. Strangely, he began to think of it as a good luck charm.

"Hey! What are you doing over there?" he called out, running toward her, wondering why he felt like a restless elementary schoolkid the night before a field trip. Each step he took reminded him of the anticipation he felt when going to a gaming store the day some massive studio's new RPG was slated for release.

Index still took no notice of him.

Touma Kamijou stifled a smile at her very Index-like reaction (or lack thereof).

It was only then that he realized Index had collapsed in a pool of blood.

* * *

"...Uh...?"

Surprise wasn't his immediate reaction. Rather, it was hesitation.

He hadn't noticed sooner, given that the throng of cleaning robots obstructed her, but her back had been lacerated by a horizontal slash near her waist. The wound had the appearance of having been inflicted by a sword, as if a ruler and X-Acto knife had been employed to carve a straight line through a cardboard box. Her neatly cut silver hair was dyed crimson.

"Human blood" wasn't his immediate association.

The gap in reality between this moment and the one immediately preceding rendered Kamijou dazed. *Deep, deep red...ketchup? Right before she collapsed from hunger, she must have used the last of her strength to drink some ketchup*. He summoned the happy imagery, trying to smile.

He tried to smile, but he couldn't.

Of course not.

The three cleaning droids, squeaking back and forth in short movements, dabbed at the mess on the floor, attempting to use their mops to arrest the spread of the crimson pool. The slick red draining from Index's body...It was as if they were using a dirty cloth to stanch the wound. It was as if they were vacuuming out her insides.

"S...stop, stop! Shit!!"

Finally, Kamijou's eyes adjusted to the reality before them. He tried grabbing the janitorial droids gathered in a frenzy around the gravely wounded Index. They were constructed to be stupidly heavy in order to prevent theft, and they had quite a bit of horsepower, too, so peeling them off was no simple task.

Of course, the automatons were only cleaning the "mess" expanding across the floor, and they diligently avoided any direct contact with Index. But in Kamijou's mind, these were termites come to feast around a festering wound.

Despite the adrenaline fueling him, Kamijou knew a single robot was too heavy and powerful for him to peel off, much less three of them. When he focused on one, the other two went for the "mess."

He couldn't even budge these stupid toys.

Despite being the man who could kill even God.

Index was silent.

Her motionless lips were purple from blood loss. Whether or not she was even breathing was questionable.

"Damn it, damn it!!" Kamijou shouted impotently. "What the hell? What the hell is this?! Who the hell did this to you, damn it?!"

"Hm? Oh, that would be us sorcerers."

The voice behind him was not Index's.

Kamijou turned his whole body toward the elevators as if he were about to take a swing at someone... but it wasn't the elevator... The figure seemed to have emerged from the emergency stairwell.

The Caucasian man was almost two meters tall, but his face looked younger than Kamijou's.

His age... was probably the same as Index's, so fourteen or fifteen. His height was a trait of foreigners. His clothes... looked like something a priest might wear: jet-black vestments. However, there probably wasn't a soul in the world who would call *this* guy "Father."

Perhaps because he was standing upwind, Kamijou caught a whiff of some way-too-sweet perfume, even though the man was more than fifteen meters away. His shoulder-length blond hair was dyed red like a sunset, and silver rings lined up on each of his ten fingers like brass knuckles. Gaudy earrings hung from his ears; a cell phone strap peeked from his pocket; a lit cigarette lounged in the corner of his mouth; and, to top it all off, a tattoo resembling a bar code was engraved under his lower right eyelid.

Neither *delinquent* nor *priest* seemed to adequately describe this guy.

But the man standing in the walkway clearly emanated an abnormal aura.

Kamijou felt like the normal rules governing life no longer held sway, as if some entirely new set of physical laws had taken hold. He felt icy tentacles floating in the air around him.

Neither terror nor anger took hold as his immediate reaction.

It was once again hesitation. Hesitation and unease. It felt as if his wallet had been stolen in a foreign country where he didn't speak the language. It was that kind of hopeless isolation. The icy tentacles probing the air took hold of his heart. It was then that he understood.

This was a sorcerer.

This world was now an abnormal environment—a world that supported the existence of sorcerers.

He could tell at a glance.

He still didn't believe in sorcerers.

But this person clearly existed outside his world—the world in which his common sense applied.

"Hmm? Hm-hm-hm. My, this certainly turned into a big show." The sorcerer looked around, making the cigarette twitch in the corner of his mouth. "I heard that Kanzaki had cut her, but... Well, I *thought* things were okay because there wasn't any blood trail, but..."

The sorcerer noted the cleaning robots gathered behind Touma Kamijou.

Index had probably been cut somewhere else and had run for her life. When she arrived here, her strength had failed. The droids in the meantime had neatly wiped away the trail of her fresh blood on the floor.

"But why...?"

"Hmm? Oh, the reason she came back here? Who knows? Maybe she forgot something. Now that I think of it, she'd been wearing a hat when we shot her in the back yesterday. I wonder where she dropped that?"

The sorcerer in front of Kamijou had said that she "came back."

In other words, he'd been trailing Index the whole day. And he knew about her forgetting the hood of her habit, the Walking Church.

Index had mentioned something along the lines of them searching for its magic power.

So the sorcerers were tracking her by searching for the abnormal power inside her habit. Kamijou was pretty sure she'd also told him that they would know the Walking Church had been destroyed and that its signal had been cut off.

But Index should have understood what that meant, too.

She knew all of it, but she still tried to rely on the defensive prowess of her Walking Church.

And why on earth would she come back? Why did she need to retrieve one piece of the shattered, ineffectual habit? If the entire Walking Church had been rendered useless by Kamijou's right hand, then the hood would serve no purpose.

...All right, then are you willing to follow me into the depths of hell?

Suddenly, everything clicked into place.

Kamijou remembered that he hadn't actually touched the last piece of the Walking Church. In other words, there was still magic power inside it. Index had figured that the sorcerers would use it to find her.

So she'd braved the danger and come all the way back here.

"...You idiot."

She hadn't needed to do that. It was entirely his fault that the Walking Church had been destroyed, and he'd kept the hood in his room on purpose. She had no duty, obligation, or authority to protect his life.

But she wouldn't have been satisfied unless she returned.

She'd been compelled to turn back for Touma Kamijou, a complete stranger whom she'd only known for thirty minutes.

She risked her life so that he wouldn't get involved in her battle with the sorcerers.

She wouldn't have been satisfied unless she'd come back.

"...You absolute idiot!!"

Index wasn't moving an inch. It ticked him off for some reason.

She had told him that his rotten luck was caused by his right hand.

He was unconsciously erasing even fishy abnormal forces like the divine protection of God and the red thread of fate.

If he hadn't carelessly touched her with his right hand, if the Walking Church hadn't been destroyed, then she wouldn't have come back.

No, whatever. No need for excuses like that.

Whatever his right hand was or wasn't, and whether or not the Walking Church was shattered, she hadn't needed to come back.

If Kamijou hadn't wanted that connection...

If he had only returned the hood to her properly when he'd had the chance...

"Hmm? Hm-hm-hm? Aww, don't look at me like that." The sorcerer's cigarette twitched again. "I wasn't the one who cut *that*, and I'm sure Kanzaki didn't mean to make *it* bleed so much. Everyone knows about the Walking Church's absolute defense, of course. It shouldn't have put a scratch on her... Man, how on earth did it end up getting broken, anyway? The Dragon of Saint George hasn't been resurrected yet, so it's impossible for a Papal-class barrier to be torn down."

His words ceased, as if he'd been muttering to himself, and his smile disappeared.

But that was only for a moment. He started wiggling his cigarette again right away, as if he'd suddenly remembered the motion.

"Why... why?" Kamijou stammered, without thinking, without expecting an answer. "Why? I don't believe in magic or fairy tales, and I can't understand you sorcerers. But don't you know the difference between good and evil? Don't you have something or someone you want to protect...?"

He had no right to say that. He was nothing but a fraud.

He'd allowed Index to go off on her own, returning to his daily life.

But he just had to say this, no matter what.

"You all bullied a young girl, chased her around, and made her bleed like this... Can you really claim to have any sense of justice, you dick?!"

"I already said I wasn't the one who made it bleed; it was Kanzaki."

The sorcerer cut him off plainly, unaffected by Kamijou's words in the slightest.

"Anyway, I'm picking up what I came here for, blood-soaked or otherwise."

"Picking... up?" Kamijou didn't understand.

"Hm? Oh, I see. I thought everything had been leaked, since you knew what a sorcerer was. *It* was probably scared of getting you involved in all this." The sorcerer exhaled a drag of cigarette smoke. "That's right, I'm here to pick *that* up. To be more precise, I'm not here for *that* but for the 103,000 grimoires it possesses."

...Again with the 103,000 grimoires.

"I see, I see! You probably don't understand, since religion is pretty weak in this country," the sorcerer explained, his tone sounding bored despite the smile on his face. "Index Librorum Prohibitorum—translated, it means the 'index of forbidden books.' It's a list of wicked, evil books, published by the Church, which it insists would corrupt your soul if you read so much as a little. Even if the Church were to send out word that such dangerous books were in circulation, one of the vile tomes could still end up in someone's hands if the unwitting fool didn't know the title. So *that* was transformed into a crucible of poisonous knowledge, containing 103,000 'bad books.' Ah, you want to be careful. For someone like yourself, living in a country with feeble religious views, just looking at one would cripple you for life."

Kamijou heard the sorcerer's diatribe, but Index still didn't have a single book with her. If she did, he would have been able to see it under her habit; he had, after all, seen every line on her body. Someone carrying a hundred thousand books wouldn't be able to walk anyway. A hundred thousand books was enough to fill an entire *library*.

"Qu-quit messing with me! Where the hell are they then, huh?!"

"They're there. In that thing's *head*—in its *memory*," the sorcerer replied smoothly, as if stating the obvious.

"Have you ever heard of eidetic memory? Apparently, it's an ability that lets you memorize anything the instant you see it. It's also called perfect recall. Like a human scanner." The sorcerer smiled, still bored. "We're not talking about our occult magic or your scientific supernatural abilities here. It's just a trait. *It* went to places around the world like the British Museum, the Musée du Louvre, the Biblioteca Apostolica Vaticana, the ruins of Pataliputra, the Château de Compiègne, and the Mount Saint Michael Academy and 'stole' the grimoires sealed there *using only its eyes*. It is a library of grimoires."

There was no way Kamijou could believe that.

He couldn't believe in these grimoires or this "perfect recall" stuff.

But it wasn't important whether or not they were true. In reality, there was a person right in front of him who'd slashed a girl's back because he *believed* it was true.

"Well, the girl herself can't train her magical power anyway, so she's harmless." The sorcerer rocked the cigarette around in the corner of his mouth gleefully. "The Church must have a few ideas of their own, preparing a stopper like that...Well, I'm a sorcerer, so it doesn't have anything to do with me. Anyway, those 103,000 books are dangerous things. So before it falls into the hands of someone who'll *use* it, I've come here to place it under my protective custody."

"Pro...tection?"

Kamijou was flabbergasted. With this crimson landscape before him...What did this man just say?

"That's correct. That's right. *Protective* custody. However much common sense or goodwill she may have, she probably won't be able to stand up to torture and drugging. Thinking about handing over a girl's body to people like that just breaks your heart, doesn't it?"

"..."

Something in Kamijou's body was quaking.

It wasn't simply anger. Goose bumps were breaking out on his arms. The man he was looking at truly believed that *he* was always right. *His* way of life was beyond reproach, never seeing his own faults. It made Kamijou feel as if he'd just lowered himself into a bathtub filled with thousands of slugs. A chill surged through his entire body.

The phrase *lunatic cult* came to mind.

This sorcerer was hunting people out of blind faith, without any sort of grounding or logic behind it. When Kamijou thought about that, his nerves snapped.

"You . . . you bastard!!"

His right hand felt as if it surged with an intense heat, and it made a cracking sound as if resonating with his anger.

His legs, once glued to the floor, moved faster than he could think. His dull body made of flesh and blood shot toward the sorcerer like a bullet. He clenched his right hand so tightly it seemed as if his intention was to crush his own fingers in his grip.

His right hand was useless. It couldn't take down a single delinquent, or raise his test scores, or make him popular with girls.

But his right hand was very convenient because it was capable of punching the shit out of the prick standing in front of him.

"This would be the part where I introduce myself as Stiyl Magnus, but I suppose I should call myself Fortis931 at this point." He casually twisted his mouth, his cigarette dancing at the motion. He muttered something to himself before declaring to Kamijou as if bragging about his cool black cat:

"That's my magic name. Not used to hearing that? Apparently we *sorcerers* mustn't reveal our true names when we are employing magic. It's an old convention, and I don't really get it."

Fifteen meters separated them.

Touma Kamijou halved that distance with just three steps.

"Fortis would be something like 'strong' in Japanese. But the etymology doesn't matter. What's important is that I used this name to introduce myself. For sorcerers like me, it's less of a magic name and more of a . . ."

Touma Kamijou continued sprinting down the hall another two steps.

The sorcerer kept smiling despite that, as if to imply that his opponent wasn't someone capable of wiping away his smug grin.

"... a killer name, perhaps?"

The sorcerer, Stiyl Magnus, removed the cigarette from his mouth, flinging it aside with his fingers.

The butt flew horizontally, slid along the metal railing, and struck the wall of the neighboring building.

An orange trail of light outlined the trajectory of the cigarette, and when it hit the wall, embers scattered.

"Kenaz..."

As Stiyl spoke, the orange afterimage suddenly exploded with a loud roar.

The straight line became a flaming sword, as if expelled by a fire extinguisher filled with gasoline.

Kamijou could hear the paint on the walls boiling and changing colors. It sounded like a photograph being roasted with a lighter.

He hadn't even touched the sword, but Kamijou felt as if just looking at it would scald his eyes. He stopped automatically and covered his face with both hands.

His legs weren't moving. It was as if they'd been hammered into the floor with a *bang*.

Kamijou experienced doubt.

The Imagine Breaker could erase any abnormal power with a single touch. Even the *biri biri* girl Mikoto's Railgun, a power conceivably capable of destroying an entire nuclear bunker with a single blast, was no exception.

Still...

Kamijou had never seen a supernatural force besides metahuman abilities.

What about magic?

Would his right hand work against magic—a completely unknown equation?

"... Purisaz Naupiz Gebo!" The sorcerer laughed through the hands Kamijou was using to cover his face.

As he laughed, the white-hot fire blade seared into Touma Kamijou's side.

On contact, it lost its cohesion and erupted indiscriminately like a volcanic torrent. It spewed waves of heat, flashes of light, explosions, and black smoke all around him.

"Did I...overdo it?"

Stiyl scratched his head. The scene had just been bombed. He'd checked the surrounding area for bystanders beforehand. Most of the students who lived in this dormitory were probably out enjoying the first day of summer break, but if there were any friendless shut-ins still around, things would get complicated.

A screen of black smoke and fire blanketed Stiyl's view.

But he didn't need to bother checking to know what had happened. His attack was a hellfire that burned at 3,000 degrees Celsius. Apparently above 2,000 degrees, human skin liquefies instead of burns, so the kid was probably a thick mass of ooze stuck to the wall like gum, just like the metal railing that had melted like molten candy.

He exhaled, realizing that his decision to draw the boy away from Index had been justified. If he had used the wounded Index as a shield, things would have gotten a little ugly.

...But he couldn't pick up Index like this.

Stiyl sighed. He wasn't able to cross the flame-strewn hallway to retrieve her. If there were an emergency flight of stairs on the other side of the hallway, he could reach her, but if she melted in the flames while he went around, it wouldn't be funny.

He shook his head, trying to work out how to proceed. As if he could see through the smoke, he spoke up again. "Excellent job. Congratulations, but I'm sorry for your loss. If that's all you've got, then you couldn't win even if you tried a thousand times."

"*Who* couldn't win a thousand times?"

The sorcerer froze, startled, at the voice emerging from the hellfire.

With a massive roar, the fire and smoke obscuring the area were suddenly dispelled in a gust.

It was as if a tornado had suddenly appeared in the center of the conflagration and blown everything away.

In its place stood Touma Kamijou.

The railing had liquefied like candy, the paint on the floor and walls was peeling, and the fluorescent lamps mounted on the ceiling dripped, having melted from the heat. In the eye of the inferno, the boy stood there, wholly unscathed.

"...Jeez, of *course*. What was I so scared about?"

Kamijou uttered the words from the corner of his mouth, sounding bored.

"...This was the right hand that destroyed Index's Walking Church."

He honestly understood nothing about magic.

He didn't grasp the mechanism of the thing or what was going on if he couldn't see it. Even if someone explained it to him from start to finish, he probably wouldn't understand half of it anyway.

But stupid as he may have been, he did know one thing.

In the end, it was just another abnormal power.

The scarlet flames he'd expelled hadn't been completely extinguished.

A neat circle of flame still crackled around Touma Kamijou.

"Out of the way."

With this command, Kamijou touched the 3,000-degree-Celsius flames. The lot of them were expunged simultaneously, like birthday candles on a cake blown out with a single breath.

Kamijou sized up the sorcerer in front of him.

The conjurer was confused at this clearly unanticipated turn of events, as any human would be.

Oh, this **"thing"** *was* human.

If he was punched, he'd feel pain, and if he was sliced with a hundred-yen X-Acto knife, he'd bleed red blood. **He was *just a human being*.**

Kamijou's knees no longer knocked, and his body was no longer frozen.

He moved his limbs just as he always had.

It moves!

"...Wha—?"

Stiyl, on the other hand, almost backed away from the unexplainable phenomenon he had witnessed.

Considering the environment around him, there was no way his attack could have misfired. Then was the boy's body strong enough to withstand temperatures over 3,000 degrees Celsius? No, he wouldn't even be human, then.

Touma Kamijou didn't stop to consider Stiyl's confusion.

He slowly advanced one step at a time, clenching his hot right fist into a boulder.

"Damn!!"

Stiyl waved his arm horizontally. Another flaming sword appeared, just like the first, and slammed into Kamijou with explosive force.

A detonation. Flames and black smoke everywhere.

But when the fire and brimstone dissipated, the boy was still standing. Again.

...Could he... be using magic?

Stiyl considered the possibility but immediately discounted it. There was no way there was a sorcerer in a foolish country that thought Christmas was a day for dating.

Besides...besides, if Index, who had no magical power, joined forces with a sorcerer, she'd have no need to flee. That was how dangerous her memories were.

Possessing those 103,000 grimoires was fundamentally different from having something like a nuclear missile.

Living things die; a suspended apple falls; one plus one equals two...These were inviolable laws. But in fact, they *could* be broken, rewritten, and born anew. One plus one would become three, apples would fall up, and the dead would rise.

Sorcerers called those the "demon gods."

Not a demon from hell, but rather a sorcerer who had trespassed into God's domain.

A demonic god.

But he could sense no magical power from the boy before him.

As a sorcerer, he could tell with a glance. This kid didn't have the smell of someone from Stiyl's world.

Then why?

"!!" As if in denial of the frigid sensation shooting down his spine, he conjured a third flaming sword and rammed it into Kamijou.

This time, there wasn't even an explosion.

The instant Kamijou touched the fiery blade with his right hand, the entire thing shattered like glass, melted into the void, and disappeared. He did it as casually as swatting a fly.

His bare right hand, with no magical enhancement, had destroyed Stiyl's 3,000-degree hellfire blade.

"…Uh."

For some reason—no real reason he could think of—something popped up in the back of Stiyl's mind.

Index's habit, the Walking Church, was Papal class, which meant it was absolute. The power of its defensive barrier rivaled those of London's cathedrals. As long as the legendary Dragon of Saint George hadn't reappeared, destroying it was *absolutely* impossible.

But Kanzaki had sliced Index. That meant the Walking Church had been shattered beyond recognition. But by who? And how?

"……"

Touma Kamijou was already right in front of him.

If he took one more step, he could punch the sorcerer.

"MTWOTFFTO, IIGOIIOF (one of the five elemental components of the world, the great fire of beginning)…"

A nervous sweat broke out all over Stiyl's body. Because the living *thing* in front of him, wearing a summer school uniform, looked human. He sensed something else coiled within the boy's body, beyond the blood and the meat. Stiyl felt his very spine shaking.

"...IIBOL, AIIAOE (it is born of life, and it is the arbiter of evil)...

"...IIMH, AIIBOD (it is mild happiness, and it is the bane of death)...

"...IINF, IIMS (it is named fire, and it is my sword)...

"...ICR, MMBGP...!! (I call thee into reality; masticate my body for great power...!!)"

The chest of Stiyl's vestments immediately expanded like a balloon; the buttons flew off, popped from within.

As the flame devoured the oxygen with a roar, a giant ball of flame leaped from his clothing.

It wasn't just a ball of fire.

Inside those brightly blazing flames was a core of thick petroleum-like bile. The core had the shape of a man. It looked like a human being covered in suffocating black oil, like a bird fallen victim to an oil spill. It burned incessantly.

Its name was Innocentius, the Witch-Hunter King—and its very name implied certain death.

The flaming giant with inevitable death's moniker spread its arms and charged at Touma Kamijou like a bullet.

"Out of the way."

Boom.

Delivering a simple backhand with all the annoyance of brushing through a spiderweb, Touma Kamijou swatted away the sorcerer's final trump card. The oil-drenched human figure of the flaming giant sprayed out in all directions, like a water balloon pierced by a needle.

"...?"

Just then, Kamijou decided not to take that last step forward. There was no logic behind his decision.

Stiyl, whose last gambit had been eradicated, was smiling, and that made Kamijou hesitate to take that final step carelessly.

Suddenly, he heard a squelching sound of jelly coming from every direction.

"Wha—?!"

He took a step back, startled, and the black spray reconstituted itself in midair, once again taking on human form.

If he had taken that last step, the giant's flames would have encircled his entire body for sure.

Kamijou was confused. If what he knew about the Imagine Breaker was true, then it could destroy even divine miracles with a single blow. As long as this sorcerer's attack was a magical, abnormal power, he should have been able to completely nullify it with a touch.

Inside the flames, the thick, oily figure writhed, changed shape, and transformed into the silhouette of a person gripping a sword with both hands.

No, that was no sword. It was a giant cross, more than two meters tall, that looked as if a man could be crucified on it.

The demon wielded the cross in a large arc, bringing it down on Kamijou's head like a pickax.

"…!!"

Kamijou grunted and immediately shielded himself from the blow with his right hand. After all, he was just a regular high schooler. He lacked the combat skills to see an attack like that coming and avoid it.

The cross collided with his right hand with a giant metallic *crash*.

This time, it didn't disappear. Instead, Kamijou felt a slight resistance to his grip, as if he was squeezing a rubber ball. The enemy used both hands, but Kamijou could only use one. Millimeter by millimeter, the flaming cross edged closer to his face.

Panicked, Kamijou only just barely noticed. This ball of fire, Innocentius, the Witch-Hunter King, was definitely reacting to his Imagine Breaker. But no sooner was it destroyed than it managed to resurrect itself. The interval between destruction and revival was probably no more than a hundredth of a second.

His right hand was trapped.

If he freed it for even an instant, he would immediately be reduced to ash.

"...Runes."

Touma Kamijou heard something.

He couldn't turn around to look behind him due to the crisis in front of him consuming his attention, but he immediately recognized the voice.

"...Twenty-four letters that describe mysteries and secrets. A magical language employed by Germanic tribes since the second century, in which Old English **is said to have its** roots.

He knew it was Index, but he couldn't believe it.

"Wha...?"

How can she be speaking so calmly when her body's wrecked and drenched in blood?

"Attacking the Witch-Hunter King will have no effect. The walls, floor, and ceiling. As long as the inscribed runic seals surrounding us remain intact, it will be reborn ad infinitum."

Touma Kamijou was only barely able to stop the cross's advance by bracing his right wrist with his left hand.

Very slowly, he turned his head.

A solitary girl was still curled up where she'd fallen. But he couldn't call *that* Index. Its eyes were like a machine's, utterly devoid of emotion.

With every word it spoke, blood seeped from the wound in its back.

It was unfazed, nothing more than a system created for the sole purpose of explaining magic.

"Y-you're Index... right?"

"Yes. I am the library of grimoires belonging to Necessarius, the Church of Necessary Evils, the 0th parish of the English Puritan Church. My proper name is Index Librorum Prohibitorum, but you may call me Index for short."

Kamijou felt a tremendous chill as he considered the life of the library of grimoires—the index of prohibited books. It was nearly enough to make him forget about Innocentius, who was currently trying to kill him.

"If introductions are complete, I shall return to my explanation of runic magic... To put it simply, it is comparable to the moon reflected in a pool of water at night... No matter how much one slices the water's surface with a sword, the moon will remain unaffected. If you wish to cut the moon reflected in the water's surface, you must first direct your blade toward the real moon floating in the night sky."

Index's lesson complete, Kamijou finally remembered Innocentius, the enemy before him.

So then, this wasn't the *actual* aberrant force? Then it was like destroying a photograph but not the negatives. Unless he destroyed the actual abnormal power manifesting the flame giant, it would continue reviving forever. Was that what she meant?

At this point, Kamijou still didn't believe what she was saying.

Even though he'd come this far, his common sense still screamed that magic wasn't real.

Anyway, with his right arm sealed by Innocentius and his body immobilized, he couldn't have tried a different tactic even if he wanted to and asking the blood-soaked Index for help seemed an unlikely prospect.

"Ashes to ashes..."

He flinched. Behind the giant, flaming god, Stiyl manifested another sword in his right hand.

"... and dust to dust..."

A second sword, this one white-hot, appeared soundlessly in his left.

"... Squeamish bloody rood!" shouted the sorcerer, charging forward, his blazing sabers held parallel to the ground like a pair of scissors, as if he intended to slice through the flaming giant as well. Kamijou stood helpless to defend with his right hand occupied by the Witch-Hunting King.

Oh, shi— Gotta run!!

Before Kamijou could so much as scream, the two fiery swords collided with the infernal behemoth and ignited it like a bomb, engulfing Kamijou in the conflagration.

7

The fire and smoke cleared to reveal a hellish landscape.

What had remained of the metal railing had been pulverized like a jawbreaker, and even the floor tiles slopped around like molasses. The paint peeling off the walls had turned to ash, revealing the concrete beneath.

The boy was nowhere to be seen.

But Stiyl did hear the sound of footsteps retreating beneath him.

"...Innocentius."

The sorcerer's voice came in a whisper. The sporadic flames once more assumed a human form, which leaped over the railing in pursuit of the footsteps.

Subjectively, Stiyl was surprised. It wasn't a problem. Just before the explosion, his swords had cleanly bisected the flaming giant, and Kamijou had released his right hand, hurling himself over the rail.

As he fell, the boy had likely grabbed hold of the railing the next floor down and pulled himself onto the walkway. He'd done so without a safety net of any kind, pulled it off by sheer force of will. Stiyl considered it reckless.

"But, hmm..."

The sorcerer smiled to himself. Index's 103,000 grimoires had revealed the weakness of his runes. As she'd said, his runic magic was fueled by a series of seals he'd inscribed. If those seals were removed, any magic drawn from them, no matter how powerful, would be instantly annihilated.

"But *so what*?" he reassured himself, relaxing. "You can't do it. You can't possibly destroy every single rune I've inscribed on this building."

"I thought...! I thought I was...! I thought I was really gonna die!!"

Kamijou's heart was still attempting to pound its way free of his chest following his seventh-story free fall without a lifeline.

He sprinted down the straight passageway, looking around. He didn't wholly trust Index's assessment. At this point, his immediate concern was to get the hell away from Innocentius and regroup.

But faced with the reality confronting him, he couldn't help but shout, "Damn it! What the hell is going on?!"

The problem wasn't that he didn't know *where* in the sprawling dormitory the runes were inscribed. Actually, he'd already found some of them: on the floor, on doors, on fire extinguishers. Paper scraps the size of credit cards hung everywhere he looked, just like in the fable of Hoichi the Earless.

He didn't want to think about her puppetlike expression, but according to Index, the magic was like an interference field, and those paper runes were antennae emitting the interference signals. *I... think? Can I even pull them all off? There are, like, thousands of these stupid paper antennae things all over the place.*

Rumble! He heard the thunderous roar of oxygen being absorbed as the humanoid flame descended over the metal railing.

"Crap!"

If he got caught again, he wouldn't be able to hold it back. Kamijou immediately ducked into the emergency stairwell running alongside the walkway. Even there, as he hopped farther and farther down the steps, more of the runic characters or whatever could be seen hanging in nooks and crannies on the stairs and ceiling—suspicious shreds of paper with symbols on them, adhered everywhere with cellophane tape.

They'd obviously been mass printed on a copy machine.

How does something that stupid even work?! Kamijou thought angrily. Considering it further, though, he realized that fortunes could still be read using free giveaway tarot cards that came with *shoujo* manga, and it was certainly possible to mass-produce copies of the Bible at a printer.

This whole occult thing is totally cheating...

Kamijou wanted to cry. There were tens of thousands of these runic seals stuck all over the building. Could he actually find every single one? Even if he tried, couldn't Stiyl just start hanging up more to replace them?

His thoughts were cut short as Innocentius began descending the stairway after him.

"Damn!"

He gave up on the stairs and exited onto the next floor's hallway. The flame giant collided with the pavement, scattering embers everywhere, and bounded down the passage in pursuit.

The hall was completely straight. At his usual speed, Kamijou wouldn't be able to shake Innocentius.

". . . !" Kamijou grunted and glanced at the entrance to the emergency stairs. A label informed him that this was the second floor.

Rumble! Innocentius barreled straight for him to restrict his right hand.

"O-oaaahhh!"

Kamijou neither used his right hand, nor did he retreat farther. He hurdled the second-floor railing with everything he had.

As he fell, he realized that asphalt and a handful of bicycles were waiting below.

"Ack, aahhhh!!"

He barely managed to land between bikes, but the hard asphalt below couldn't be avoided. He tried bending his legs to absorb the impact, but he still heard his ankles crack. They didn't feel broken—maybe because he had only fallen two stories—but there was definitely some damage.

Rumble! The flames overhead released another massive roar as they sucked up oxygen.

"?!"

Kamijou rolled aside, scattering the bikes, but nothing happened.

. . . ? He looked up, confused.

Innocentius, the Witch-Hunter King, was still stuck at the second-floor guardrail. It watched him closely, still rumbling. It was like an invisible barrier blocked its path, preventing it from pursuing him.

The runes must only have been hung in the dormitory. Kamijou would be able to escape Stiyl's magic by just abandoning the building entirely.

Now that he'd figured out the rule behind it, he felt like he'd gotten a handle on the aspect of the invisible system of magic. Just like the supernatural abilities with which he was familiar, magic was governed by its own laws. It wasn't like the crazy enemy mages in RPGs who could do whatever they wanted with a single spell.

Kamijou sighed.

Now that his life wasn't in immediate peril, all his strength drained from him. He had to take a seat on the ground. This wasn't fear—what settled over him was more like lethargy. He even started thinking, *If I just ran away like this, I'd be safe, right?*

"That's right! The police...," Kamijou mumbled to himself. Why hadn't it occurred to him before? Academy City's police force was a special anti-esper team. Wouldn't it be better to contact them instead of almost getting himself killed?

He fished around in his pockets but remembered that he'd stepped on his cell phone that morning.

Instead, he searched the street in front of the dormitory to find a public phone.

Not to run away.

Not to run away.

"...All right, then are you willing to follow me into the depths of hell?"

Her words once again pierced his heart like an arrow.

He hadn't done anything wrong. He wasn't doing anything wrong, was he?

He couldn't be expected to plunge into the depths of hell with a complete stranger he'd only known for thirty minutes, even if she *had* returned for his sake in what was essentially the same circumstance.

"Damn, fine then... If I don't want to follow you into the depths of hell, then..." Kamijou grinned. "I guess I'll just have to pull you out of there, now won't I?"

It was about time to believe her.

He didn't care about the rules governing magic. He didn't know what was going on behind the curtain. After all, did he need a blueprint of a cell phone in order to send a text message?

"...Well, it's no big deal once you've figured it out, is it?"

If he knew what needed to be done, all that was left was to do it.

Even if it ended in failure, it was better than sitting around doing nothing.

Rumble! The crushed metal guardrail, glowing orange, fell toward him. He rolled to the side in a panic.

He wanted to settle everything in a cool way, but in order to save Index, he needed to do something about that flame freak, Innocentius, first. The problem at hand was figuring out what to do about tens of thousands of runes.

Could he actually peel off every single scrap of paper taped throughout the building?

"...Man, it's kind of weird that the fire alarm isn't going off, what with all the smoke."

Kamijou muttered to himself inadvertently. Suddenly, he stopped.

The fire alarm?

All at once, every fire alarm in the building suddenly started blaring.

"?!"

Stiyl looked up at the ceiling amid the storm of warning sirens.

The sprinklers overhead started spraying man-made rain without wasting a second. He'd made sure to inscribe a command to Innocentius instructing it not to touch any security sensors, since things would have gotten exponentially more complicated if the fire department had been called in. That meant that Touma Kamijou probably pulled the fire alarm.

Was he trying to douse the Witch-Hunter King's flames?

"..." It was such a ridiculous notion that Stiyl couldn't bring himself to laugh. But for that ridiculous reason, he was now getting soaked. He was so frustrated that he felt his brain might explode.

He glared with venomous hatred at the bright red fire alarm on the wall.

Setting them off was simple enough, but from here, he probably couldn't do anything to stop them. Most of the dorm's residents were out enjoying their summer vacation, but he preferred not to be around when the fire department arrived.

"...Hmm."

Stiyl assessed his surroundings and decided to pick up Index and make a hasty retreat. His objective being her retrieval, there was no need to obsess about annihilating Kamijou.

Besides, the boy would probably be a pile of white or black ash, incinerated by Innocentius on automatic, by the time the fire department reached the scene.

...I wonder if the elevators have stopped.

He'd heard that elevators were designed to shut down in case of emergencies. The prospect made him even more miserable. He was on the seventh floor and had no desire to lug a limp body down seven flights of stairs. Even if it was just a little girl, it would be exhausting.

So he was relieved when he heard a *ding* like a microwave timer sound off behind him.

But he quickly came to his senses.

Who's that? Who'd be in the elevator?

He'd already verified that the dormitory was deserted with its residents out gallivanting for an evening of summer vacation. Who on earth was it? Moreover, what would possibly motivate someone to use an elevator *now* of all times?

The Dumpster of an elevator opened its doors with a low rumble. He heard the echo of a single footstep splash against the drenched floor.

Stiyl turned slowly.

He couldn't fathom why his insides were trembling in fear.

There, at the end of the hallway, stood Touma Kamijou.

... What? What happened to Innocentius? I set him on autopilot to run that kid down, didn't I?

Thoughts chased one another through Stiyl's mind in a whirl. Innocentius functioned not unlike a fighter jet with a payload of cutting-edge missiles. Once locked onto a target, it was relentless; no matter where the victim might try to run or hide, the 3,000-degree colossus would melt through anything in its path, be it a simple wall or a sheet of metal. There was no way a target could evade it just by running around.

And yet there stood Touma Kamijou.

Audaciously. An invincible, savory, worthy opponent. The *fated* enemy. There he stood.

"So, those rune things were 'carved' into all the walls and floors, right?" Kamijou called out, soaking in the artificial rain. "... Man, you really got me there. You're really a piece of work, you know that? Had you actually carved them with a knife, I'd have been screwed. You can brag about that."

He raised his right arm and pointed above his head with his index finger.

The ceiling. The sprinklers.

"... No! Not a chance! A 3,000-degree inferno can't be snuffed out like that!"

"Stupid! Not the fire—**those stupid things you stuck all over my house,** dumbass!"

Stiyl worked it through. The tens of thousands of runes he'd planted around the dormitory had been printed on copy paper.

Paper dissolves in water. Even kindergarteners knew that.

If the building was flooded with water, it wouldn't matter how many thousands of runic characters he'd inscribed. You wouldn't need to run around taking them all down. You'd just have to press a button, and every last sheet would be destroyed.

The muscles in the sorcerer's face contorted involuntarily.

"Innocentius!"

The next moment, the flame giant *crawled* into the passageway behind Kamijou, crushing the elevator door as if it were made of gingerbread.

With every raindrop, its fiery body *hissed* as the water evaporated—the sigh of a beast.

"Ha...ha-ha. Aha-ha-ha-ha-ha-ha! Amazing! You truly are a tactical genius! But you lack experience. Copy paper isn't toilet paper, you know. **It's not weak enough to be melted by a little water!**"

The sorcerer spread his arms wide, smiling tremendously, and barked, "Kill him!"

Innocentius, the Witch-Hunter King, hoisted his arm back like a hammer.

"Out of the way."

That was all he said. Kamijou didn't even bother to turn around.

Blorp. The boy reached around to initiate contact between his right hand and the fire titan. Accompanied by a frankly hilarious sound, it went *kablooey* every which way.

"Wha—?!"

Stiyl Magnus's heart skipped a beat.

Innocentius was gone, and he wasn't coming back. Oozing blobs of pitch coated the walls, the floor, and the ceiling, doing little more than wriggling around a bit.

"Th-that's...impossible. How? How?! My runes aren't wrecked yet...!"

"What about the ink?"

It seemed as if it took five years for Touma Kamijou's words to reach his ears.

"Even if the copy paper isn't ruined, the ink starts to run when the water hits it, right?" Kamijou explained calmly. "...Though it seems like it didn't destroy *every one* of them."

Fragments of Innocentius continued to writhe.

The black blobs dissipated, one by one, with every spritz of artificial rain from the sprinklers, in much the same way that the ink on the talismans hung around the building was being diluted and sapped of its power.

One by one, they faded, until finally the last of them melted away and was gone.

"In... nocentius... Innocentius!" the sorcerer wailed, but he was pleading with someone who'd already hung up the phone on him.

"All right, then."

Kamijou's statement made the mage's entire body twitch.

His feet took one step toward him.

"In... no... centius...," the sorcerer called out. The world did not answer.

A foot advanced a second step.

"Innocentius... Innocentius, Innocentius!" the sorcerer bellowed. The world held firm.

Touma Kamijou shot at him like a projectile.

"Ah... ashes to ashes, dust to dust, squeamish bloody rood!" the sorcerer howled. Neither flaming giant nor fiery sword appeared.

Touma Kamijou's feet finally closed the gap. He took one more step in...

...and made a fist with his right hand.

With his completely ordinary right hand. A right hand that was useless against anything but abnormal powers. A right hand incapable of taking down a single delinquent, of raising his test grades, or making him popular with girls.

But his right hand was very convenient.

After all, it was capable of punching the shit out of the prick standing in front of him.

Kamijou's fist plowed into the sorcerer's face.

The mage's body spun around like a top, and the back of his head collided with the remnants of the metal guardrail.

CHAPTER 2

The Miracle Worker Grants Death

The_7th-Edge.

1

It was night. The sirens of fire trucks and police cars blared through the main road before passing on.

The student dormitory had apparently been close to empty, but setting off the alarms and sprinklers had quickly drawn a large crowd of fire trucks and curious bystanders alike to the scene.

After disabling the hood transmitter in his apartment, Kamijou carried it out. He could have left it functional and thrown it somewhere random to try and throw off her pursuers, but she stubbornly insisted on keeping it.

He came to an alley and let out a *tsk*. He still cradled the blood-soaked Index in his arms. The ground was dirty, and he couldn't let it come in contact with her open wound.

He also couldn't call an ambulance for her.

Generally speaking, Academy City disliked outsiders. It was for this reason that the city was surrounded by a wall and under constant surveillance by three dedicated satellites. Even a truck attempting to park behind a convenience store needed a specific ID or it would be denied access.

Index had no identification. If she was hospitalized here, news of her presence would spread like wildfire.

They were up against an entire organization, after all.

If they were attacked in a hospital, it would only mean more victims. In the worst-case scenario, she could be attacked in the middle of surgery with no means of defending herself.

"... But I can't just leave you here like this."

"I'm... fine... okay? If I can just... stop the bleeding..." Index's voice was weak and devoid of the mechanical tone it bore during her rune lesson.

Even Kamijou knew she was lying. Her wound went way beyond bandages. After fights, he usually performed first aid on himself so he wouldn't have to tell anyone about them, but even he didn't know what to do when faced with this kind of trauma.

At this point, there was only one hope.

He couldn't believe it, but he had no choice but to.

"Hey, hey! Can you hear me?" He lightly slapped Index's cheek. "Isn't there some kinda magic healing spell in those 103,000 books of yours?" Magic, in his mind, was just a bunch of attack and healing spells like in RPGs.

Index herself lacked magical power, so she couldn't wield it. But if Kamijou, who used an abnormal power, had her walk him through it, maybe...

Her breathing was shallow, likely more a result of blood loss than pain. Her pale lips moved in reply.

"... There is, but..."

He experienced a moment's elation, right up to the "but."

"You wouldn't... be able to." She exhaled a little. "Even if I taught you the technique... and you performed it perfectly..." She groaned. "Your... power would get in the way."

Kamijou looked at his right hand, speechless.

The Imagine Breaker... It had completely dispelled Stiyl's flames, so it might end up nullifying the healing magic, too. "D-damn it! Not again... This stupid hand...!!"

He had to call someone, then. Maybe Blue Hair, or maybe that *biri biri* girl, Mikoto Misaka. A few faces came to mind, tough ones who could handle trouble like this.

"...?" Index was silent for a moment. "Ah no...That's not what I meant."

"?"

"It's not your right hand...it's because you're an esper," she explained, her body shivering despite the sweltering heat, as if she was on a wintry mountain. "Magic...isn't meant to be used by espers like you...Magic...Its techniques and rituals are for those without gifts...who still want to achieve what...those blessed with talent can."

He fought the urge to shout, *Why are you lecturing me* now?!

"Do you understand...? The circuits in those who have talent... and those who don't...are different. Someone with abilities can't... use a system created for...those without it..."

"Wha...?" He was at a loss. Espers like him acquired their supernatural endowments by **forcing their irregular brain circuits to open** using drugs and electrical stimulation. Their bodies actually **were** fundamentally different.

But he couldn't believe it. No, he didn't *want* to believe it.

There were 2.3 million people living in Academy City, and every single one of them was taking a Curriculum for developing their powers. Even if a person didn't look like one, and even if he or she couldn't bend a spoon despite straining his or her brain to the point of aneurism, **that only meant that the person was a useless esper and was still built differently than normal people.**

In other words, there wasn't a single person in the city capable of applying the magic she could teach him or her.

There was a way to save this girl but nobody to help her.

"God...damn it..." Kamijou gritted his teeth like a beast. "This is insane. There's no way! What the hell is this?! Why is this happening...?!"

Index was shaking badly.

The thought that plagued him the most was that **she was about to pay the price for his own powerlessness**.

"What is this talent good for?" he spat. It couldn't even save an isolated, suffering girl.

But it wasn't like he could think of anything else. None of the 2,300,000 students living in this city could use magic—it was a fundamental incompatibility.

"...?"

Lamenting this, Kamijou suddenly realized he was looking at it wrong.

Students?

"Hey, you said that a normal person with 'no talent' could use magic, right?"

"...Huh? Yeah."

"And there's no catch, like you have to have *magical* talent specifically, right?"

"No, it's fine...If you can prepare the method, then...I think even a middle schooler would be capable..." Index thought for a moment. "...Though of course, if you mess up the steps, your brain circuits and nerves will all get fried...But I'm Index, so it's okay. There's no problem."

He grinned.

Like a wolf preparing to howl, he looked up at the moon.

It was true that the 2.3 million students living in Academy City were all undergoing Development for their supernatural abilities.

But, on the other hand, the ones who were developing those powers—the teachers—should just be normal humans.

"...That teacher can't be sleeping yet."

One teacher's face floated into Touma Kamijou's mind.

His homeroom teacher: a single, 135-centimeter-tall instructor who, though she was an adult, looked good in an elementary school backpack.

Komoe Tsukuyomi.

He used a public phone to call Blue Hair to ask where Miss Komoe lived. (His phone, of course, having been ruined this morning. Why Blue Hair would have a clue where their teacher lived? Unknown. Likely stalker.) Afterward, he set off, hoisting the limp Index on his back.

"Here we are..."

It was about a fifteen-minute walk from the alley.

How should I put it? Despite Miss Komoe looking like a twelve-year-old, her place was a wooden two-story wreck of an apartment that looked so old it could have survived the bombings of Tokyo. After he noticed the washing machine outside next to the road, he figured there wouldn't be any indoor showers or baths.

Normally, Kamijou would have been able to crack jokes about this place for ten minutes, but at the moment, he wasn't in the mood for levity.

He ascended the terribly rickety metal stairwell and checked the nameplates on the doors one by one. He walked to the farthest entrance on the second floor and finally found the name TSUKUYOMI KOMOE written in hiragana.

Ding-dong, ding-dong. He rang the doorbell twice, then tried with all his might to kick the door in.

Slam! Kamijou's foot collided with the doorframe, producing a tremendous noise.

However, the entry didn't budge, not even a little. His big toe cried out in protest. "~~~!!" His faithful rotten luck was still right by his side.

"Yes, yes, the door is tough to defend against newspaper salesmen! I'm opening it now, okay?"

I should have just waited patiently, he thought, tears in his eyes. The ingress opened, and Miss Komoe, clad in baggy green pajamas, poked her head out. Her face was relaxed. She probably couldn't see the wound on Index's back from there.

"Wow, hello, Kami! Did you start a paper route?"

"Where on earth do paperboys carry nuns on their backs when they go out soliciting?" Kamijou demanded angrily. "I've got a bit of a problem here, so I'm coming in. Excuse me!"

"W-wait wait wait wait!"

He tried to squeeze past Miss Komoe, but she frantically blocked his path.

"I, umm, would like you to stay out. Well, I mean, it's not like it's a huge mess or that there're empty beer cans on the floor or a mountain of cigarette butts or anything like that!"

"Miss!"

"What is it?"

"...Try telling that joke again after you see what I'm carrying on my back."

"I-it wasn't a joke... Wait, gyaah!!"

"You just realized now?!"

"I couldn't see her injury because you're so big, Kami!"

Miss Komoe was rattled, flustered by the unexpected sight of blood.

Kamijou pushed past her and made his way into the apartment.

The room looked as if an old man addicted to horse racing lived there. A ton of overturned beer cans lay scattered all over the old tatami flooring, and a mountain of cigarette butts was piled in a silver ashtray. He didn't know what kind of joke this was, but in the middle of the room sat a tea table that an angry drunk would love to upend.

"...What can I say... You weren't joking after all, were you?"

"It might seem strange for me to ask, but do you dislike women who smoke?"

That isn't the issue here! Kamijou thought, sizing up his homeroom teacher, who looked all of twelve. He kicked some of the random beer cans on the floor to one side and cleared a space. There was no time to get out a futon to spread over the battered tatami, though he had reservations about putting Index on it.

He rested Index facedown so her open wound wouldn't touch the filthy floor.

The torn fabric made it difficult to see the laceration directly, but a deep red seeped from it like crude oil.

"Sh-shouldn't we call an ambulance? Th-there's a phone right over there, you know?"

Trembling terribly, Miss Komoe pointed to a corner of the room. For some reason, it was a black rotary-dial phone.

"...My life force... my mana... is ebbing away with the blood loss."

Startled, Kamijou and Miss Komoe looked at Index.

She was still on the floor, her limbs sprawled across the tatami. Her face rested on its side. But her eyes were open, not unlike a broken doll's.

They were colder than pale blue moonlight, quieter than a clock's gears.

Her gaze was perfectly calm, calmer than any human eyes should have been.

"...Warning. Reading from chapter two, verse six. Mana drainage via blood loss has reached critical levels. Forcing awakening by the Automatic Clerk, John's Pen...If the current state continues, calculated using international standard time displayed as per Big Ben in London, my body's mana levels will fall below required minimum in approximately fifteen minutes, and I will die. Please follow the instructions I am about to give and take appropriate measures."

Miss Komoe, her heart in her throat, looked at Index's face.

It's only natural, thought Kamijou. This was the second time for him, but he certainly wasn't used to that voice.

"Now, then..."

He studied his teacher's face, lost in thought.

If he suddenly asked her something like, *Please use magic!* in this situation, she would answer, *Kamijou, this is an emergency. We can't make believe we're magical girls! Teacher is too old for this!*

How on earth should he explain the situation, then?

"Hmm. Teacher, Teacher, I'll keep this short because it's an emergency. I need to tell you a secret, so come over here."

"Okay."

Kamijou gestured that she should come as if he was calling a puppy. She drew closer, utterly earnest.

I'm sorry, Kamijou mouthed in apology to Index.

With one swift motion, he unveiled the horrendous wound concealed beneath her shredded clothing.

"Eek!!" Miss Komoe's body quaked. That was to be expected, too.

Despite being the one pulling off the fabric, even he was shocked by the severity of the injury. It was a surgical line starting near her waist, as precise as if someone had used a straightedge and a box cutter. Beneath the sanguine fluid, pink muscle and yellow fat had been exposed, and still deeper, Kamijou thought he saw something hard and white—her backbone.

The "lips" around the mouth of the wound were turning a pale blue, not unlike a person's actual lips after too long in a pool.

Ugh...Steadying himself from a bout of dizziness, he slowly replaced the sopping fabric.

When the cloth made contact with the lesion, Index was unfazed. Her eyes were like ice.

"Teacher."

"Huh? What is it?!"

"I'm going to go call an ambulance now. While I'm doing that, I need you to listen to what this kid has to say and do whatever she asks. Just definitely don't let her fall unconscious. As you can see, this girl is part of a religious order. I'll leave things in your hands."

Telling Miss Komoe was what she needed—it would prevent her from denying magic altogether. In any case, what was important wasn't that his teacher treat the injuries properly anymore, it was to keep Index talking no matter what.

Miss Komoe's face was still pale, and she nodded with grave seriousness.

...The one problem was how Kamijou would waste time outside.

If he called an ambulance before the ritual was complete, the treatment would be interrupted. This meant he couldn't call for paramedics.

But that left him without a reason to excuse himself. He could always use the black phone in the room, dial 117, and pretend to ask the automated voice for an ambulance.

That wasn't the problem.

"Hey, Index," Kamijou prompted softly. "Is there, uh, anything I can do?"

"...Not possible. The best course of action in this situation is for you to evacuate the area."

He involuntarily clenched his right hand into a fist, to the point that it hurt, at her completely transparent, straightforward answer.

There was nothing he could do.

His mere presence was enough to nullify the healing spell.

"...Okay, Teacher. I'm gonna go run to a public phone."

"Uh...what? Kami, there's a phone right over—"

He ignored her and left the room.

He bit down on his teeth, frustrated with himself for being unable to help.

Kamijou sprinted through the darkened streets.

Despite being the man who could kill even God, his right hand couldn't protect a single person.

"...What is the current Japanese Standard Time? I would also like to know the date."

"It's July twentieth, eight thirty in the evening, but why?"

Index paused.

"...You do not appear to have checked a clock, so are you certain that is the correct time?"

"There isn't a clock in here in the first place. Teacher's internal clock has a second hand, so there's no problem!"

"..."

"There's nothing to be skeptical about. In fact, I hear horse jockeys have their internal clocks fine-tuned down to a tenth of a second. If you can regulate your eating and exercise habits exactly, you can manage it," Miss Komoe explained matter-of-factly. Even though she wasn't an esper, she was certainly a resident of Academy City. Everyone here had a unique understanding of science and medicine compared to the outside world.

Index, still facedown on the floor, moved only her eyes and looked out the window.

"...Judging by the stars' position and the angle of the moon...the location of Sirius matches your time with a margin of error of 0.038. I will now confirm. The current Japanese Standard Time is July twentieth at eight thirty PM, correct?"

"Yes. More precisely, it's fifty-three seconds after that… Hey, wait, you shouldn't get up!!"

Index rose, compromising her shattered body even further. Miss Komoe, panic-stricken, tried to push her back to the floor, but one glance from Index stopped her in her tracks.

The gaze was neither scary nor sharp.

It was as if her eyes had flipped a switch. Gone was any trace of emotion.

They were completely devoid of life.

It was as if her soul had departed her body.

"It does not matter. Regeneration is possible." Index headed for the tea table in the center of the room. "… We are in the end of Cancer for half the night, from eight o'clock to midnight. Cardinal direction is west. Under Undine's protection, the angel's role shall be Hailwime…"

"Eek!" Komoe caught her breath, startled. Her quiet cry echoed throughout the room.

Index had begun drawing a diagram of some sort on the tea table with her blood-soaked finger. Even if Miss Komoe didn't know what a magic circle was, she could tell it was something religious. She was fainthearted, unable to utter even a sound. She stared at the sigil, feeling overwhelmed.

Inside the circle of blood, which took up the entire tea table, was a pentagram.

However, it was bordered by tightly packed words in a language that belonged to another country. They were likely the same words Index was currently muttering to herself. She had asked for the current constellation and time because the characters that needed to be inscribed were dependent on the time and season.

Her movements as she conjured this magic betrayed none of the frailty of a person suffering grievous injury.

Her concentration seemed to have sequestered her sensation of pain for the time being.

The quiet sound of blood dripping from her back sent a chill down Miss Komoe's spine.

"Wh-wh-wha-what is that?"

"Magic," Index replied hollowly. "From this point, I will borrow your hands and body. If you do as I direct, no one will need to deal with any misfortune, and you will avoid any malice."

"Wh-what are you talking about?! Just lie back down on the floor and wait for an ambulance! Uhh, bandages! Where are the bandages? With a laceration this severe, we should stop the flow of blood by binding the area near the arteries—"

"It is impossible to wholly arrest my blood loss with that degree of treatment. I do not quite understand the meaning of the word *ambulance*, but can that completely stanch this wound within fifteen minutes and further replenish my body with the requisite amount of mana?"

"..."

She was right. If Komoe was to call an ambulance now, it would take ten minutes to get here. Bringing her back to the hospital would take twice that, and it wasn't as if she would be healed the moment they arrived. She didn't really understand what the girl meant by the occult term *mana*, but there was no doubt that just closing the gash wouldn't replenish her stamina.

Even if she immediately sutured the trauma with a needle and thread, the pallid thing would lose all her strength and die before she could recover her vitality, wouldn't she?

"Now, please."

Index issued her instruction, her eyes inscrutable.

A thin line of saliva tinged with fresh blood trickled from the corner of her mouth.

Though her tone had been neither commanding nor ghastly, her very sedate composure made the girl all the more terrifying. It was like watching a broken machine moving, wholly unaware that it had been destroyed. She couldn't help but feel as if Index's wound grew more severe with every action she took.

...It looks like if I resist, she'll get a lot worse... Miss Komoe heaved a sigh. Her eyes still weren't expecting to see magic, of course. But

Kamijou had made it absolutely clear that she should keep the girl talking and awake.

The only thing she could do now was to try not to excite her in any way and hope that Kamijou returned with an ambulance as soon as possible, followed by a miraculous bit of triage by trained medical professionals promptly thereafter.

"So what should I do? Teacher isn't a magical girl, you know?"

"I thank you for your cooperation. First, give me that, that... What is that black thing?"

"? Oh, that's a video game memory card!"

"???... All right, that will do. Anyway, please place that black thing in the center of the coffee table."

"It's more like a tea table, but okay."

As directed, Miss Komoe positioned the memory card in the center of the tea table. After that, she surrounded it with a mechanical pencil lead case, an empty box of chocolates, and two small books on their ends. Finally, she lined up a pair of little toy figurines.

What is this? wondered Miss Komoe. But Index was the picture of seriousness, although she still looked poised to collapse at any moment.

"What is this? You said magic, but... aren't we just playing with dolls?"

When Miss Komoe considered the configuration more closely, it appeared to be a miniature diorama of that very room. The memory card was the tea table, the two books standing on their ends were her bookshelf and closet, and the two figurines were positioned precisely where she and the injured girl stood in the room. Glass beads later scattered around the tea table perfectly mirrored the beer cans on the floor.

"Ingredients are inconsequential. A magnifying glass can be composed of glass or plastic, but either material will facilitate closer observation... If an object's shape and function are approximate, the ceremony may proceed." Index spoke in little more than a whisper, sweating profusely. "In any case, I request that you carry out my instructions in exacting detail. Should you fail to maintain the proper order, your nerves and brain circuits may burn out."

"???"

"I mean that in the event of failure, your body will be minced and you will die. Please be careful."

Miss Komoe coughed in surprise. Index ignored her and continued.

"I shall call down an angel and create a temple. Please chant after me."

What came out of her mouth next were sounds, not words.

Miss Komoe attempted to imitate the pitch as if humming a tune, without dwelling on its meaning.

And then…

"Eek?!"

All of a sudden, the figurines on the tea table began "singing" as well. One of them even mimicked her "eek" in real time. The figure vibrated; its vibration replicated her voice in the little effigy as if it were being transmitted along a string to a paper cup.

The only reason Miss Komoe didn't completely lose it and dash out of the room was because she was a resident of Academy City, renowned home to more than 2.3 million espers.

Co-habitating with more than 2.3 million espers in this city would have driven any normal person mad by this point.

"Link established," came Index's voice in stereo, both from her own mouth and from the figure on the tea table. "The temple created on the table has been linked with this room. Essentially, anything that transpires inside this room will do so on the table, and anything that transpires on the table will do so in this room."

Index pressed lightly on one of the legs of the tea table.

Concurrently, the entire apartment trembled with a loud *creak*, the impact shaking Miss Komoe's legs.

It was then that she noticed that the stagnant air inside her apartment was becoming as clean and crisp as a forest morning.

She didn't see anything resembling an angel anywhere, though. She could only sense some sort of invisible presence. Her skin broke out in goose bumps all over. She felt as if thousands of eyes were observing her from every angle.

All of a sudden, Index shouted, "Now, imagine a golden angel with the body of a child! A beautiful angel possessed of a pair of wings!"

Defining the active field was a crucial element of magic.

For example, if one throws a pebble into the ocean, it doesn't create a very big ripple. However, if one drops a pebble into a bucket of water, it causes large and powerful rings. Magic was similar. First, a specific field had to be defined in order to isolate the area the magic was to distort.

A Guardian is a temporary deity placed within this small, predesignated world.

If they could visualize a concrete Guardian, stabilize it, and control it the way they wanted, mysterious manipulations would be easier to perform within the field.

But Index skipped the explanations. Miss Komoe found herself unable to envision an angel. The words *golden angel* only brought to mind the chocolate brand where you search for the silver or gold angel on the box for a prize.

As if aligning itself with Miss Komoe's fuzzy vision, the presence surrounding them steadily began losing its form. A revolting sense that she was sinking in fetid mud at the bottom of the swamp came over her.

"Anyway, picture it! We are not calling an actual angel. It is only a gathering of mana, an invisible power. Its form is dictated by your will!" Index's voice, which had been calm and mechanical before, was now as pointed as icicles. Maybe she'd reached the end of her patience.

Miss Komoe shut her eyes in surprise at Index's sudden one-eighty and, rattled, chanted to herself:

"...A cute angel, a cute angel, a cute angel..."

Desperately, she vaguely visualized a female angel from a girls' manga she'd read long ago.

Suddenly, it felt as if...the invisible, muddy *thing* floating around the room started to coalesce, as if it were being blown into a human-shaped balloon.

Miss Komoe nervously opened her eyes a bit.

...Wait, we're not calling an actual angel, are we?

The very moment she doubted it...

Bang! The human-shaped mud ball burst, sending it spewing through the room.

"Kyaah!"

"...Form stabilization has failed." Index looked around with pointed, observant eyes. "...If we can at least guard this temple with the azure water Undine, there will be no problem...Now proceeding." Her words were optimistic, but her eyes weren't smiling at all.

Miss Komoe couldn't help but tremble. She felt like a child who had hidden a test on which she'd performed poorly, only to be found out by her parents.

"Chant after me. One last phrase, and it will be over."

Index's command was sharp so as to allow no time for the teacher to panic, although her concentration was on the verge of breaking.

Index, Miss Komoe, and the two figurines standing on the tea table sang.

Within the diorama, the back of Index's effigy liquefied with an amorphous gurgle.

It sounded like rubber being melted by a lighter. As the toy's back lost its integrity, the lines and curves vanished, becoming smooth, before ultimately cooling and reassuming their form.

Miss Komoe's heart froze in fear.

Index sat facing her on the opposite side of the tea table.

The diminutive teacher lacked the fortitude to dare stand and examine her back.

The frightening girl's pallid blue face dripped with greasy sweat.

Miss Komoe couldn't glean any pain or suffering from her glassy eyes.

* * *

"...Confirmed replenishment of mana and avoidance of life-threatening crisis. Returning John's Pen to dormancy."

Soft light suddenly returned to Index's gaze as if a switch had been flipped.

A warm atmosphere enveloped the room as if a cold hearth had been kindled.

That was how gentle and warm Index's eyes were, the eyes of just a simple girl.

"Now...we'll return the descended Guardian, destroy the temple, and it will be over." Index almost smiled, but her lingering pain seemed to get in the way. "That's all magic is. Just like how *dog* and *canine* have the same meaning...Even without relying on glass, we have transparent plastic umbrellas these days! Tarot cards are the same. You can even use the free prizes that come with *shoujo* manga to tell fortunes, as long as the pictures and number of cards are right."

Index was still sweating heavily.

However, Miss Komoe grew even more frightened, worried that she had somehow worsened Index's condition.

"I'm fine..." Index looked as if she might collapse at any moment. "This is basically a cold. I just need to rest and regain some stamina, and I'll heal right up. The actual wound is already closed, so don't worry."

The moment she finished speaking, her body wavered and fell to one side. The figurine on the tea table fell over as well. The tea table shook a tiny bit, consequently rocking the entirety of the linked room with a powerful tremor.

Miss Komoe was about to rush to the other side of the little table when Index started to sing.

The teacher imitated her as before, and after they had finished, the peculiar atmosphere of her apartment reassumed its familiar air. Just to make sure, Miss Komoe tried wobbling one of the table legs a little. Nothing happened.

"Thank goodness," Index mumbled, closing her eyes in relief.

Anyone would feel some relief at having survived such a close brush with death, right? thought Miss Komoe. However, the nun went on:

"Thank goodness he didn't have to bear that cross…"

Startled, she looked at Index.

"…If I'd died here, **he probably would have had to bear it for the rest of his life.**"

Index stopped speaking and closed her eyes as if enjoying a dream. Passed out in the wake of a brutal assault and even during that enigmatic ceremony, she had never worried for herself. The wounded girl had only been thinking about the boy who'd carried her all this way.

Miss Komoe was incapable of that kind of selflessness. She didn't have anyone to think about that way.

So she wanted to ask just one thing.

Index was already asleep, and so she was certain the girl wouldn't hear her question. That's why she asked.

But eyes still closed, the girl answered her nonetheless: "I don't know.

"I've never thought about anybody in that way before, so I don't know what that feels like. But when he fought for me with no regard for his own life while facing the sorcerer, I thought that even if I had to crawl, I needed to get him away from there. But after Innocentius chased him off…when he came back for me, I was so happy I almost cried.

"I don't get it at all, but when we're together, nothing ever goes the way I think it will.

"But that unpredictability is so fun and makes me happy.

"I don't understand what kind of emotion that is, though."

She smiled with her lids comfortably lowered, as if enjoying a merry dream, and this time, Index fell asleep.

2

The following morning, she really did develop flu-like symptoms.

Index sprawled on the floor beset by a fever and headache. It wasn't a virus, since her nose wasn't running and her throat didn't hurt. She was just recovering her life force. So in other words, no matter how much cold medicine she took to bolster her immunity, it wouldn't do jack.

"...So? Why aren't you wearing pants exactly?"

Index, a moist towel on her forehead, thrust one leg out from under her futon toward Kamijou, unable to bear the heat. Even though above she wore light green pajamas, he could see her thigh almost up to her waist. Her skin was brilliant, eye piercing, and pink from her fever.

Miss Komoe dunked the now-lukewarm towel from Index's forehead into a washbowl and glared at Kamijou.

"...Kami, Teacher thought that those clothes were just a bit too much."

"Those clothes" meaning Index's safety pin–bespotted white habit.

Kamijou was in full agreement with her on that point, but Index had grown accustomed to wearing the habit. When they'd taken it away, she'd looked like an annoyed cat.

"...So, wait. Why does a beer-guzzling, chain-smoking adult have pajamas that fit Index perfectly? Just how much of an age difference is there between you two?"

Miss Komoe (age unknown) was flabbergasted, and Index butted in as if to cover for her. "...Don't belittle me. I think these pajamas are a little tight around the chest, even for me."

"Wha...? Impossible! You're bugging me! You're making fun of me too much. I won't take that!"

"Wait, you *have* a chest for pajamas to be tight around?!"

"..."

The two ladies glared at him. Kamijou defensively fell back on his soul-crushing, head-to-floor bowing pose.

"That's what I thought. By the way, Kami, how are you and this girl related?"

"She's my younger sister."

"That's an obvious lie! She's a silver-haired, blue-eyed foreigner!"

"It's not by blood."

"...Are you a pervert?"

"It was a joke! I get it! I know that dating an in-law is improper, but real is illegal! Aw, jeez!"

"Kami," she prompted, adopting her educator's tone.

He shut his mouth. *Well, of course Miss Komoe would want to know what's going on here.* After all, he'd carried a complete stranger into her apartment—one with a more than slightly suspicious sword wound in her back—after which she'd been forced to take part in some weird magic hokum that she didn't understand.

It was probably too much to ask for her to turn a blind eye to it all.

"Teacher, can I ask a question?"

"What is it?"

"Are you asking because you want to report it to the police or the board of directors of Academy City?"

"Yep," Miss Komoe answered promptly, nodding. She hadn't hesitated a second to inform a student she would sell him out. "I don't know what kind of trouble you two have gotten yourselves into"—Miss Komoe smiled—"but if it's something that happened in Academy City, the responsibility of dealing with it falls on us teachers. It's an adult's duty to see to the welfare of children. Now that she knows you two were endangered, Teacher will not keep quiet about it!"

Such was Komoe Tsukuyomi's declaration.

Even though she had no strange powers, no physical strength, and no authority...

She spoke with such directness, such *correctness*, as if she were a blade of integrity speeding directly for its target.

I'm no match for her, confessed Kamijou to himself.

Although he was on the back half of two decades' worth of life experience, he couldn't think of anyone else quite like this teacher.

There weren't even characters like her in movies or TV dramas anymore.

"Miss Komoe, if you were a complete stranger, I'd involve you as much as necessary, but since I owe you for the magic, I don't want to involve you any further."

Kamijou decided to be straight with her.

He didn't want to watch *another* person shielding without expecting anything in return, only to see her get hurt.

Miss Komoe paused briefly.

"Hmm. Teacher won't stand for such meaningless posturing, okay?"

"…? Wait, Teacher, why are you getting up? Where are you going…?"

"I'm granting you a stay of execution. Teacher is going to the supermarket to buy breakfast. Until I get back, Kami, figure out what you want to tell me and how to explain it clearly, okay? And…"

"And?"

"Your teacher might get wrapped up in her shopping and completely forget about it. When I get back, make sure you initiate the conversation yourself like an adult, okay?"

Kamijou thought she was smiling.

The door slammed shut, leaving Kamijou and Index alone.

…Maybe she did that for us.

For some reason, when he pictured her childlike, plotting face, he got the feeling she might actually forget everything by the time she returned.

Still, if he ever needed her advice later, she'd probably jump down his throat, shouting something along the lines of *Why didn't you tell me before?! I had completely forgotten!* before gladly hearing him out.

He sighed and turned back to Index, still resting on the futon.

"…Sorry. I know this isn't the time to be worrying about being cool."

"No, you were right." Index shook her head slightly. "We shouldn't involve her any further… Besides, she can't use magic anymore."

"?" Kamijou frowned.

"Grimoires are dangerous, you know. The uncommon sense written with them breaks the laws of nature. They're from a different world. It's not that they're good or evil, but that they're poisonous to this world."

Index explained that just gleaning knowledge from the other world could destroy someone's mind. *Maybe it's something like trying to force a program to run on an operating system it's not designed for*, Kamijou wondered, trying to come up with an analogy he could understand.

"...My mind is protected by the Church's defenses. Sorcerers strive to exceed their human limitations—and common sense itself—to reach their goal, which drives them mad. But since Japan is so unindoctrinated in terms of religion, if a Japanese person...If she recited that incantation one more time, she'd be done for."

"H-huh..." He tried to not let his shock show on his face. "That's kind of a shame. I thought we could just make Teacher into an alchemist or something. I know about alchemists. They can turn lead into gold, right?"

Secretly, his source for this factoid was an item-oriented RPG whose main character was an alchemist.

"...They can perform Ars Magna, but...if you gathered the necessary ingredients and tools these days, in terms of Japanese currency...it would cost around, umm, seven trillion yen."

"..Well, that's completely pointless," Kamijou grumbled, as if his soul had left his body. Index smiled.

"...Yep, it is. The only people who'd be happy you did it would be nobles."

"But, hmm. When you really think about alchemy, what *is* it even? What's the principle behind it? To convert lead into gold, wouldn't you have to rebuild its atomic structure from Pb to Au or something?"

"I'm not really sure, but it's just fourteenth-century technology, you know?"

"That's cra— Wait, what? You mean rearranging atomic structure?! Am I right? Doesn't that mean you could destroy protons without an accelerator and generate nuclear fusion without a stupidly huge reactor?! Wait a second, I don't know if even the seven Level Five espers in Academy City could do that!"

"???"

"Wait, what's with the puzzled expression?! Err, umm, ahh, in terms of how amazing that would be…you could make an atomic robot or a mobile suit like it was nothing!"

"What are those?"

His fanboy fantasy was cut off at the knees.

Kamijou slumped, and Index thought she'd somehow said something very bad.

"A-anyway, even if you tried to substitute a holy sword, or magic scepter, or something like that with things from the modern world in the ceremony, there's a limit to that, you know?…In particular, the Lance of Longinus, or the Book of Joseph, or the rood—many holy relics related to God are still apparently irreplaceable, even after a thousand years, but…ow…"

She groaned after attempting to sit up too quickly in her excitement and started massaging her temples as if she were hungover.

As she settled back on the futon, Touma Kamijou looked at Index's face.

Reading just one of those 103,000 books would drive a person insane, so cramming every sentence, every *letter*, precisely into your memory…How much suffering did she have to endure?

But she had never once complained.

"Would you like to know?" she asked Kamijou, as if by way of apology despite her own pain.

Index's quiet voice, in contrast with her normally cheerful disposition, revealed her determination.

Stupid Teacher, thought Kamijou.

For his part, Index's specific situation didn't matter. Regardless of her circumstances, he wasn't going to abandon her. If he could just defeat the enemy and secure her safety, there was no need to dig into her old scars. But she still asked.

"Do you really want to know what I carry?" she inquired again.

Kamijou made up his mind and answered, "Heh, it kind of seems like I'm the priest, doesn't it?

Heh, it really does... I'm just like a priest listening to a sinner's confession.

"Why do you suppose it is," Index began rhetorically, "that even though Crossism has a singular original, you have Catholicism, Protestantism, Russian Catholic, Roman Orthodox, English Puritanism, Nestorianism, Arianism, Gnosticism...? Why do you think it fractured into so many different groups?"

"Well..." Kamijou had at least *skimmed* a history textbook, so he felt like he kind of understood why. But he hesitated to say anything in front of Index since she was the real deal.

"No, that's right." Instead, Index smiled. "It's because people mixed religion with politics. It began to fragment, oppose one another, and even started wars. Eventually, people who believed in the same God became enemies. Even though we worship the same Heavenly Father, we started to walk completely separate paths."

Of course, there were many different perspectives. Some thought they could earn money through the word of God, and others found that unforgivable. Some thought they were God's chosen people on earth, and others found that wholly unacceptable.

"... After we stopped exchanging ideas, we evolved in isolation and acquired 'individuality.' We all changed in response to a variety of factors, like the state of the nation in which one worshipped or what the climate was like." She breathed a quiet sigh. "Roman Orthodoxism believed in managing and administering the world; Russian Catholicy believed in the censorship and destruction of the occult; and English Puritanism, the order to which I belong..."

Index faltered for a moment, struggled to get out her next words.

"England is the land of magic, so..." She seemed as if she was remembering something painful. "...England focused on hunting down witches and heretics, and the Inquisition...the anti-magic culture and technology thrived.

"Even now, in the capital, London, there are public corporations that call themselves 'magic societies,' and ten times their number existed only on paper. Those organizations were originally founded to protect the citizenry from evil magicians lurking in the city but eventually devolved into a culture of slaughter and execution.

"English Puritanism has a unique sect," said Index softly, almost as if confessing her own sins. "To slay sorcerers, they needed to come up with countermeasures, and they did so by researching the magic their enemies employed. The order charged with this task was Necessarius, the Church of Necessary Evils." She spoke like a nun. "If you do not know your enemy, you cannot safeguard yourself against his attacks. But understanding his corrupt soul would inevitably lead to your own soul's corruption. Touching the diseased body of your enemy would result in your own body's infection. The Church of Necessary Evils was established to combat that corruption all on its own. And their greatest achievement was..."

"The 103,000 grimoires."

"Yeah." Index nodded once. "Magic is like a mathematical equation. You can neutralize your opponent's attacks as long as you do a good job reverse engineering it. So the 103,000 books were stuffed inside me...Because if we understand the world's magic, we should be able to neutralize all the magic in the world."

Kamijou looked at his right hand.

His right hand, which he had thought useless. His right hand, which he had rejected since it couldn't take down a single delinquent, or raise his test scores, or make him popular with girls.

But she had seen hell itself in order to arrive at this.

"But if grimoires are so terrible, can't you just burn them without reading them? As long as there are people who learn things from them, won't magicians just keep appearing?"

"...The important thing isn't the book, it's what's inside. Even if you got rid of the original, if a sorcerer who already knew what was inside passed it down to a disciple, there would be no point.

"Though that person wouldn't be called a sorcerer, but rather a wizard," she added.

So it's like data flowing through the Internet, Kamijou thought. Even if you erased the data at their source, they would still exist, being copied infinitely.

"On top of all that, grimoires are, at their core, just textbooks," Index explained painfully. "...Just reading one doesn't make someone a sorcerer. A sorcerer is someone who inserts his own arrangements and gives birth to new spells."

So instead of just data, it's more like a computer virus, always being modified.

In order to completely stamp out a virus, you need to analyze it first and then constantly come up with new vaccines.

"...Also, I said this before, but grimoires are dangerous." Index's eyes narrowed. "Just destroying a single copy requires that practiced Inquisitors sew their eyes shut to protect against the corruption of their minds. Even then, unless they regularly baptize themselves for five years, they won't escape its poison. It's impossible for a human soul to deal with the originals. The 103,000 grimoires spread around the world are so dangerous that there was no other option but to seal them away."

It was almost like handling decommissioned nuclear weapons.

No, actually, it was probably **exactly like that**. It was also more than likely beyond the predictions of the people who originally made them.

"Crap. But even so, magic is something that any normal person, aside from us espers, can use, isn't it? So wouldn't it have just spread across the world in no time?"

Kamijou recalled Stiyl's flames. If the world had turned into a place where *everyone* was able to use that kind of power... the world's foundation—common sense based on science—would collapse.

"That's… not something to worry about. Not even sorcerers' societies would bring grimoires out into the open recklessly."

"? Why not? Wouldn't they *want* more allies, so they'd be stronger?"

"That's **exactly why**. If all gun owners were friends, there wouldn't be any wars, right?"

"…"

Even if you knew about magic, that wouldn't make everyone else who did your buddy.

It was quite the opposite. They'd know all your trump cards. Magicians didn't want to create enemy sorcerers unnecessarily.

Same reason you'd want to keep the blueprints for a brand-new weapon locked up.

"Hmm. I think I got most of that." Kamijou chewed on her words. "In other words, it's like… they want the **bomb** inside your head."

The original 103,000 grimoires were scattered across the globe—she was a library full of perfect copies. Getting your hands on them would mean acquiring all the magic ever created.

"… Yeah." She sounded like someone sitting on death row. "If you used all 103,000 books, you could twist the entire world to your will. We call those people demon gods."

Not the gods of the demon world…

… but rather, people who had delved too deeply into magic, too far into God's domain…

… A real-life demon.

… *That's insane.*

Kamijou had been gritting his teeth without knowing it. He could tell just from looking at her that Index hadn't had the 103,000 grimoires imprinted on her brain because she *wanted* them. He thought about Stiyl's flames again. Index lived to prevent as many casualties as possible.

He didn't like those sorcerers who used those feelings against her, but he also didn't like the Church for calling her "corrupted." Every single side was treating her like an object, and Index had spent her whole life surrounded by people like that. But the main thing he didn't like was how, regardless, she continued to put everyone else first.

"...I'm sorry."

Even Kamijou didn't fully understand what he was so angry about.

But her apology set him off.

He flicked Index's forehead lightly.

"...Would you quit this nonsense already? Why the hell'd you keep quiet about all this important stuff until now?"

Index completely froze under his glare. He was baring his teeth at her. Her eyes widened as if she'd made some sort of huge mistake, and her lips worked frantically.

"But...I didn't think you'd believe me, and I didn't want to scare you, and, umm..."

Looking as if she was about to cry, Index's voice grew quieter and quieter, to the point that Kamijou could barely hear the last part. He just barely managed to make out: "Because I didn't want you to hate me."

"That's...the dumbest thing I've ever heard!!" Something inside him snapped. "You're looking down on me, assigning me a value! Stop doing that! Church secrets? One hundred and three thousand grimoires? Yeah, I guess they're amazing, and crazy, and they're so absurd I can hardly believe any of it *now*.

"However!" Kamijou paused for a moment.

"That's all it is, right?"

Somehow Index managed to open her eyes even wider.

Her little mouth struggled desperately to produce words, but nothing came out.

"Don't underestimate me. What, you were thinking just because you memorized 103,000 books that you were creepy or something?! Did you think that just because some sorcerers came along that I'd abandon you and run away? That's bullshit. If I wasn't prepared for that, I wouldn't have picked you up in the first place!"

As he berated her, he finally understood why he was so mad.

All he wanted was to be able to *help* Index somehow. He didn't want to see her hurt anymore. That was all. But she'd always been the one trying to shield him from harm; not once had she asked him to protect her. He hadn't heard her say "Help me" so much as once.

It was mortifying.

It was really, really mortifying.

"...Trust me a bit. Don't try to pigeonhole me; you don't know me."

That was all it was. There was no reason for him to leave, even if he'd been powerless, even if he was just a normal guy.

Of course there wasn't.

Index looked up at Kamijou for a while, absorbed, but...

Sob. Suddenly, tears filled her eyes.

It was like the ice had melted.

Her lips impatiently quivered, having trouble holding back the emotions she'd pent up. She pulled the futon up to her mouth and bit it. Had she not done that, her tears had gotten so big that he was sure she would have started wailing hysterically like a kindergartner.

It probably wasn't just what he'd said.

Kamijou wasn't *that* full of himself. He didn't think his words alone could have moved her so much. It was more likely that he'd triggered something else in her, something that she'd held inside for a long time.

In spite of the painful realization that no one had likely said any kind words like that to her for a long time, he was still a little happy he finally got to see Index being weak.

But he wasn't some pervert who got off on girls crying.

In fact, he was completely embarrassed by himself.

If Miss Komoe walked in on them right now without any sort of context, she'd probably tell him to go jump off a cliff.

"Ah, uhh, okay. Look, I've got my right hand, so sorcerers don't stand a chance!"

"...But," she sobbed, "you said you had makeup classes."

"...Did I?"

"You most certainly did."

The girl's memory seemed perfect. Well, she *could* memorize every letter in 103,000 books, after all.

"Don't you dare start apologizing for interfering with my life or something. I don't give a damn about makeup classes. The school doesn't want to create more dropouts. If I cut makeup classes, I'll just have to go to makeup *makeup* classes. I can put it off as long as I want."

Miss Komoe probably would have given him hell for saying that, but he pushed the thought aside.

"..." Index, still teary eyed, silently searched Kamijou's expression. "...Then why did you say you had to hurry and go to makeup classes?"

"..Uhh."

Now he remembered. It had been right after he'd destroyed her habit, the Walking Church, with his Imagine Breaker, rendering her completely naked. The silent tension in the room had been worse than in an elevator, and then...

"...Uh, I, uhh..."

"So you felt uncomfortable because of my presence."

"..."

"You did."

After she said it a second time, tears in her eyes, he realized it was utterly impossible to evade this.

"I'b sowwy!" Kamijou shouted, shoving his face into the floor, having instinctively dropped into his apologetic bow again.

Index sat up from the futon slowly, like a sick person would, and grabbed Kamijou's ears with both hands. Then, as if taking a bite out of a giant rice ball, she chomped onto the top of his head with all her might.

* * *

Six hundred meters away, on the roof of an office building, Stiyl took his eyes from his binoculars.

"We've found the location of the boy with Index... How is she?"

Without turning to face the lady approaching behind him, Stiyl reported:

"She's alive... but since she's alive, they must have a magic user as well."

The woman was silent. She seemed pleased no one had died, as opposed to concerned about the prospect of another enemy.

Though the woman was eighteen, she stood a full head shorter than the fourteen-year-old Stiyl.

Of course, Stiyl was more than two meters tall, which still made her taller than the average Japanese.

Her black hair was pulled back into a ponytail that reached down to her hips, and a katana more than two meters long, called the Command Sword, rested in a sheath at her side; it was the kind used for Shinto rain prayers.

However, the label *Japanese beauty* didn't seem to quite fit.

She wore worn jeans and a short-sleeved white T-shirt. For some reason, the left leg of her jeans had been cut off to reveal her thigh, and the bottom of her T-shirt was tied across her stomach, exposing her navel. Her boots reached up to her knees, and the sheath housing her katana hung from a belt like a handgun in a holster.

It dangled there as if she was the sheriff in a Western, but with a katana instead of a gun.

Neither that nor her priest robes smelling of sweet perfume could be called proper attire.

"So, Kanzaki, just what is *that*?"

"Unfortunately, I haven't been able to get much information on the boy. At the very least, that probably means he's neither a sorcerer nor an anomaly."

"What, are you gonna tell me he's *just some kid in high school*?" Stiyl ignited the cigarette in his mouth with a glance. "... Don't joke. I'm actually a sorcerer who created six powerful new characters as an addendum to the twenty-four existing runic symbols. A powerless amateur couldn't have escaped Innocentius's clutches. The world isn't that nice."

No matter how much advice he'd gotten from Index, the speed at which the kid had come up with a tactic to deal with him on the fly...Not to mention his unclassified right hand...If that passed for "normal," then Japan really was a land of mystery.

"You're right." Kaori Kanzaki narrowed her eyes. "...The real problem is the fact that someone with such high combat skills is just considered another rowdy, moronic student."

Academy City's dirty little secret was its mass esper-production system.

Although Stiyl and Kanzaki had contacted and received permission from the organization known as the Five Elements Society to enter the city, they'd kept the details about Index to themselves. Even though they were part of the world's greatest conclave of sorcerers, both in name and power, the group had decided it would be impossible for them to remain hidden in enemy territory.

"I suppose they're...blockading the information. What's more, we know Index's wound was healed using magic. Kanzaki, is there another sorcerer's cabal here in the Far East?"

At this point, they were convinced that the boy was affiliated with an organization other than the Five Elements Society.

They mistakenly assumed that another group had been aggressively going around erasing all information related to Kamijou.

"...Just about everyone should be well documented within the Five Elements Society's information net, but..." Kanzaki closed her eyes. "We're dealing with an unknown enemy, and we have no reinforcements. This is a problem."

That was clearly an erroneous conclusion. As long as Kamijou's Imagine Breaker wasn't pitted against an "abnormal power," it had zero effect. In short, it meant that **even the machines used in Academy City's physical examinations** were unable to find anything extraordinary about him. Consequently, this resulted in Kamijou's unfortunate circumstance of possessing the right hand of the strongest class but being treated like a powerless Level Zero.

"Let's assume the worst-case scenario and that this devolves into an inter-cabal magic battle. Stiyl, I hear a fatal weakness was identified, what with your runes not being waterproof?"

"I've already made up for that. I laminated the runes. I won't let him use the same trick again." Deftly performing a bit of sleight of hand as if he was a stage magician, he produced a fresh batch of runes that looked like trading cards. "This time, I won't stop at just the building; I'll inscribe a barrier inside a two-kilometer radius… I'll use 164,000 runes. The arrangements should be complete in about sixty hours."

In reality, magic isn't as simple as chanting a single incantation.

Even if it looks that way on the surface, considerable preparations must be made beforehand. The source of Stiyl's fire, for example, probably necessitated something along the lines of "soaking a silver wolf's fangs in moonlight for a decade," and even this could be considered master-level speed.

In other words, magical warfare is a battle to see through the opponents' strategies. Sorcerers assume from the outset that they've already been snared in the enemy's trap, so they read the technique and counter it. Meanwhile, the attacker predicts counterattack and adjusts his approach accordingly. This is in contrast to simple hand-to-hand melee. When considered as necessitating that one read one hundred or two hundred steps ahead of his nemesis in an ever-changing situation, magical engagement could not have been further removed from the barbaric term *combat*. It was more akin to a monumental showdown of wits.

So for any sorcerer preparing to enter into a conflict, not knowing the numbers or strength of the enemy was a severe handicap.

"…They look like they're having fun."

The rune sorcerer's observation was made while staring six hundred meters ahead without the use of his binoculars.

"Yup, it really does look like fun. That child lives as if she's always enjoying herself." Then, as if spitting out something thick and viscous, he asked, "I wonder...just how much longer do we need to keep tearing it apart?"

Kanzaki, behind Stiyl, followed his gaze six hundred meters into the distance.

Even without using magic or binoculars, her vision—which was eight times better than the average—could make them out vividly. She saw the girl, furious about something, latching her teeth onto the boy's head while he flailed about violently.

"It must be a strange feeling, don't you think?" Kanzaki asked mechanically. "For **someone who was in the same place** once before."

"...It's the usual," the flame magician replied.

Just as usual.

3

"Bath time. ♪ Bath time ♪," Index sang, carrying a water bucket with both hands and walking beside Kamijou.

She had changed from out of her pajamas, back into her safety pin–patched habit, as if she'd simply quit being sick, just like that.

Just what kind of magic did they use? Her blood-covered habit was spotless. *And that pincushion of a habit...If she put it in a washing machine, it'd be ripped apart in five seconds*, Kamijou thought. Was it possible she'd taken it apart and washed it piece by piece?

"What, was it bothering you that much? To be honest, I'm not worried about how you smell."

"Does that mean you like sweaty girls?"

"That isn't what I meant!!"

Three days had passed since her ritual, and her first request once she was finally capable of moving around freely was to take a bath.

It's worth pointing out that there wasn't a bath per se in Miss Komoe's apartment. The choice before them was to either borrow the one in the landlord's place or to go to the run-down public bath near the apartments.

After several days of various happenstances, the young boy and his companion now found themselves walking down the road, carrying their bathing supplies.

...I wonder in which century this bathing culture started in Japan. Laughing, Miss Komoe had explained about the public bath system here. She was still letting the two of them stay in her apartment without asking questions. Kamijou couldn't exactly go back to his dorm since it was marked by the enemy, so he was living the life of a freeloader.

"Touma, Touma," said Index, her voice slightly muffled as she was occupied biting the sleeve of his upper arm. The girl had a bad habit of gnawing on things, and she seemed to intend it as a gesture to draw his attention.

"...What?"

Kamijou couldn't hide his annoyance. That morning, Index had announced, "Now that I think of it, I don't know your name!" Since he'd formally introduced himself, she'd cheekily used his first name about sixty thousand times.

"Nothing. I just thought'd be funny to say your name even though I don't want anything."

Thinking herself terribly witty, she wore the expression of a child visiting an amusement park for the first time.

The way Index had attached herself to him was abnormal.

It was probably a result of the incident three days earlier. Rather than simply leaving it there and enjoying it, though, Kamijou was struggling with complicated feelings about the fact that apparently nobody had said a kind word to this girl.

"I heard from Komoe that Japanese public baths have coffee milk. What's coffee milk? Is that like a cappuccino?"

"...There's nothing that fancy. It's just a public bath," replied Kamijou. *Don't go getting her hopes up like that*, Kamijou thought.

"Hmm...but a huge bathhouse bath might be a bit of a shock for you. In England, doesn't everyone have a cramped little bathroom like the ones in hotels?"

"Hmm?... Well, I don't really know about that." Index tilted her head slightly, as if she really had no idea.

"As early as I can remember, I was in Japan. I don't really know much about how things work over there."

"... Huh. No wonder you speak Japanese fluently. If you've been here since you were a kid, doesn't that pretty much make you Japanese?"

If that was the case, things started to get a little sketchy when it came to her running for sanctuary to a church in England. He thought for sure she was heading back to wherever she used to live, but she was actually trying to get to a foreign country she'd never seen before.

"Ah no, that's not what I meant."

Index shook her head in clarification, her silver hair swinging from side to side.

"I was supposedly born and raised in London, in St. George's Cathedral. Apparently, I came here about a year ago."

"Apparently?"

Kamijou couldn't help but frown at the ambiguity.

"Yeah, 'cause I can't remember anything past a year ago."

Index smiled.

It was again the expression of a girl taking her first spin on a carousel.

Her smile was perfect, but Kamijou nevertheless sensed frustration and pain behind it.

"When I first opened my eyes, it was in an alley. I didn't know anything about myself. I only knew I had to run away. Even though I couldn't remember what I'd had for dinner the night before, words like *sorcerers* and *Index* and *Necessarius* were all flying around in my head. I was really scared..."

"... So you don't know why you lost all your memories?"

"Nope," she answered. Kamijou was clueless about psychology, but the cause of amnesia in video games and TV shows was almost always one of two things.

Either she'd suffered some kind of head injury, or her brain had sealed away her memories because they were too much for her to handle.

"Damn it ...," complained Kamijou into the night despite himself. He was livid at the magicians who'd do something like this to her, but although it accomplished nothing, he felt a recognition of his own powerlessness sweeping over him.

He realized now why Index had gone out of her way to defend and had grown so close to Kamijou. She'd been thrown into the world not knowing anyone or anything, and the first acquaintance she finally made **just happened to be Kamijou**.

He didn't think it was anything to be happy about.

He didn't know why, but **that kind of** answer immediately put him on edge.

"Huh? Touma, are you mad?"

"I'm not mad," Kamijou lied, startled.

"If I offended you, then I'm sorry, I guess. Touma, how come you're mad? Is it because of puberty?"

"... Wow, I really don't want to hear about puberty from somebody with the body of a little kid."

"Mgh. What did you say? You seem mad. Or are you doing that thing where you pretend you're mad just to confuse me? I don't think I like that side of Touma."

"Wait, you didn't like me in the first place, so quit it. I'm not hoping for something out of a romantic comedy to happen here."

"..."

"Er, what? ... Why are you giving me the puppy dog eyes, princess?"

"..."

He tried to spin the situation as a joke, but Index wasn't buying it.

Weird. This is strange. Why's Index folding her arms over her chest? Why's she tearing up and looking all hurt? And why's she biting her lower lip like that?

"Touma."

"Yes?" Kamijou replied at hearing his name yet again.

A distinct sense of ill fortune washed over him.

"I hate you."

An instant later, he had the rare experience of a girl biting the whole top of his head.

4

Index ended up scurrying off to the public bath by herself.

Down the street, Kamijou was similarly trudging alone to their mutual destination. He'd tried chasing her, but the bitter white-washed nun just darted away from him like a stray. After he'd walked a bit farther, Index would eventually come back into view, as if waiting for him. And then she'd take off again. Repeat. She was seriously acting like a fickle stray.

Well, we're both headed to the same place—the public bath—so we'll meet up at some point, he ultimately concluded, abandoning his pursuit.

Honestly, he was also afraid that someone'd see him lurking through the dark streets after an obviously frail European nun. With his rotten luck, he'd end up getting arrested, no questions asked.

"A European nun, huh..."

Kamijou played out the thought lazily as he meandered the dimly lit street alone.

I get it. If I brought Index to an English church here in Japan, she'd fly out to the Church's headquarters in London soon afterward. He wouldn't have any say in the matter. In the end, she'd undoubtedly say something like, *It was short, but thank you. I won't forget about you, since I've got, like, perfect recall and everything.*

An arrow sunk into his chest at the thought—at least that's what it felt like, but it wasn't like he had any better ideas. If he couldn't return Index to the Church's protection, sorcerers would hound her for the rest of her life. And Kamijou following her to England seemed similarly unrealistic.

The worlds they inhabited, their respective situations, and the dimensions in which they existed—they were different in every way.

Kamijou lived in a scientific world of espers, and Index lived in a magical world of the occult.

The two were as distinct as land and sea and would never coexist.

That was all there was to it.

Indeed, that was all there was to it...but for some reason, Kamijou was growing irritated, as if a fish bone had gotten caught in his thro—

"Huh?"

Suddenly, his racing thoughts went dark.

Something was...strange. He looked at the clock on the neon sign outside a department store. It was only eight o'clock in the evening. People wouldn't generally have been asleep at this hour, but for some reason, the city around him had grown exceedingly quiet. It felt as if he was standing in a forest at night.

Kamijou had a bad feeling.

Come to think of it, when I was walking with Index, we didn't pass anybody...

He kept moving forward, trying to work out what was going on.

When he stepped out onto a six-lane thoroughfare, though, that vague sense of something being out of place he'd had immediately crystallized into a clear sense that something was *wrong*.

There was no one there.

No customers were coming or going from the big department stores that lined the avenue like so many juice boxes displayed on a convenience store shelf. This road always felt crowded to him, but now it looked deserted. Not a single vehicle drove along the wide highway that now bore a striking resemblance to an airport runway. The cars parked along the street were all empty and abandoned.

It was as if he was looking down a farm road at the distant countryside.

"Don't worry. Stiyl has just inscribed Opila runes to keep people away."

Kamijou's breath caught as if he'd been stabbed through the face by a katana. The voice belonged to a woman.

He hadn't even seen her.

That isn't to say she'd been hiding in the shadows or had somehow snuck up on him. She stood ten meters straight ahead, smack-dab in the middle of the wide, runway-ish, six-lane highway, as if to obstruct his path.

He hadn't just missed her because it was dark—this was on a completely different level. She *hadn't been there* a moment ago. However, when he blinked, there she was.

"It just discourages attention from the area by making people feel like they shouldn't come. Most of the people are inside the buildings. There is no need to worry."

His body, unconsciously and illogically, pumped all the blood in his body to his right hand. There was a stinging pain in it, like his wrist had been tied with rope, which instinctively told Kamijou that this person was dangerous.

She wore a T-shirt and jeans—one of the legs of which was very boldly cut—which, by itself, was still in the realm of normal clothing.

However, a katana more than two meters long hung from her waist as if holstered, swaying with cold, murderous intent in the breeze. The body of the blade was sheathed, so he couldn't see it, but the jet-black sheath, with history carved into it like a pillar in an old Japanese house, lent credence to its authenticity.

"Touma of Kamijou...the magic slayer of God's cleansing...the kanji. It is a good, true name." For all that, she didn't show any signs of nervousness. She was as relaxed as someone making small talk. And that made her all the scarier.

"...And you're..."

"I am called Kaori Kanzaki...If at all possible, I would prefer not to give my *other* name."

"Your other name?"

"My magic name."

Kamijou took a step backward automatically, even though he'd expected the reply.

Her magic name— When Stiyl had used magic to attack Kamijou, he'd called it his "killer name."

"...So I guess that means you're with the same sorcerers' society as Stiyl."

"...?" Kanzaki frowned suspiciously for a moment. "Ah, you heard that from Index, correct?"

He offered no answer.

A sorcerers' society was hunting Index because it wanted the 103,000 grimoires. It was a group attempting to achieve the level of demon god, said to be capable of twisting the fabric of the world askew.

"To be frank," Kanzaki continued, closing an eye, "I would like to secure the girl before I have to give my magic name."

Kamijou shuddered.

He had his own ace—his right hand—but still he felt a chill run down his spine when sizing up this enemy.

"...And if I said no?" he asked anyway. He had zero reason to back down.

"Then I will have no choice." Kanzaki shut her other eye. "I will simply collect the girl after revealing my name."

Wham! A shock rocked Kamijou's feet like an earthquake.

It was as if a bomb had gone off. In his peripheral vision, the distant horizon, which should have been a blanket of bluish darkness, was tinged with orange flames. Somewhere far away. Some hundreds of meters at the extent of his vision, he saw a conflagration.

"In…dex…!!"

His enemy was an organization. And Kamijou knew the name of the flame sorcerer.

In that moment of his distraction, Kaori Kanzaki unleashed her sword.

Ten meters separated Kamijou and Kanzaki. The sword she carried was more than two meters in length. With her slim arms, it looked impossible that she could even draw the sword from its sheath.

…**It should have been.**

An instant later, as if she had swept the area with a giant laser, the air above Kamijou's head was sliced wide open. He froze in astonishment. A wind turbine behind him to his right was cleft diagonally in two as easily as slicing butter and every bit as soundlessly.

"Please, stop." The voice came from ten meters ahead of him. "If you divert your attention from me, the only thing that awaits you is death."

Kanzaki had already resheathed her two-meter-long sword. It was too fast. Kamijou couldn't even see the blade touch the air.

He couldn't move.

The only reason he was even still standing was because Kanzaki had purposely missed. That was all his brain could manage. Even that didn't seem real. This opponent was too terror inspiring for a mind to quickly comprehend.

The bisected windmill propeller behind Kamijou struck the ground with a loud *clank*.

Even though the blade's fragments crashed down immediately to his side, he *still* couldn't move.

"…!" Kamijou unconsciously gritted his teeth at the realization of how insanely sharp her blade must have been.

"I will ask once more." Kanzaki opened a single eyelid. "I would like to secure the girl before I have to give my magic name."

Her voice was unwavering.

Her tone was cold, as if she were suggesting that it was far too soon yet to be surprised.

"...Wh-what...are you...talking about?" His feet were glued to the ground. He couldn't even take a step back, much less advance.

Kamijou felt his legs trembling wildly and his stamina quickly failing, as if he had just completed a marathon.

"There's no reason for me to surrender...to someone like you—"

"I will ask as many times as necessary."

Reminiscent of some sort of computer glitch, Kanzaki's right hand blurred, momentarily disappearing.

With a blast of wind, something accelerated toward him at horrifying speed.

"?!"

He had that same mental image from before of giant laser cannons swinging in his direction.

It was a massive whirlwind created by a blade traveling fast enough to leave a vacuum in its wake.

With Touma Kamijou at the center of the typhoon, the asphalt, streetlights, and trees lining the thoroughfare at regular intervals were all vivisected as if being demolished by a construction-grade hydraulic cutter. A stray bit of concrete the size of a fist struck Kamijou's right shoulder, and that was all it took to send him flying and threaten to make him pass out.

He looked around, clutching his throbbing right shoulder, without moving his neck.

One. Two, three four five six seven...Seven linear incisions ran along the even asphalt at a distance of more than ten meters. The sword cuts, which had assailed Kamijou from random and varying directions, had gouged the street in such a way that they gave the impression of claw marks carved into a steel door by bare fingernails with such force as to tear them off.

He heard the sword ease back into its sheath.

"I would like to secure the girl before I have to give my magic name."

Kanzaki, right hand still poised on her blade's hilt, spoke in a tone unburdened by hatred or malice. It was just a voice.

Seven times. Kamijou hadn't even seen one strike, but in less than a second, she'd executed seven *iai* attacks. Had she been so inclined, she could have easily vivisected his body with those seven slashes. The seven slashes that meant certain death.

It was likely the **abnormal power** of magic. She must have possessed some sort of sorcery that both augmented her swordsmanship and extended her range some ten meters. Not to mention that she'd completed seven strikes while drawing her blade only once.

"My Seven Heavens Sword weaves these 'Seven Glints' into its attack. At this speed, it can easily slay a man seven times over in the span of a single moment. People would call it instantaneous, but certain death would be similarly accurate."

Kamijou, speechless, clenched his right hand with crushing force.

With its speed, power, and range, her slash attack had to employ some kind of supernatural force like magic. That being the case, if he could somehow just manage to touch the blade…

"Fantasy." His speculations were cut short. "I've received Stiyl's report. For some reason, your right hand can dispel magic. However, that is impossible if your right hand can't make direct contact, correct?"

…She was right. If he couldn't touch it, his right hand was useless.

It wasn't just about speed. Stubbornly (and stupidly), Mikoto Misaka always insisted on challenging him head-on with her sparky attack and her Railgun, but Kamijou couldn't even read the motion or direction of Kaori Kanzaki's phantasmagoric Seven Glints. If he tried busting out the Imagine Breaker, the seven strikes would doubtlessly slice his arm into neat, round pieces.

"I will ask however many times I need to."

Kanzaki's right hand quietly touched the hilt of the Seven Heavens Sword at her waist.

A cold sweat trickled down Kamijou's cheek.

If she decided to stop fooling around and actually moved in for the kill, there was no question he'd be hacked into eight pieces. She had a range of more than ten meters and enough destructive force to carve the trees along the road into nice, thin slices. For that reason alone, running or trying to shield himself would be tantamount to suicide.

He gauged the distance between the two of them.

It was about ten meters. If he sprinted with muscle-rending force, he could reach her in four steps.

...Move.

Kamijou desperately commanded his feet, which felt like they were covered in superglue.

"Would you please allow me to secure the girl before I have to give my magic name?"

...Mo...ve!!

Kamijou tore his foot off of the ground, inching it slightly forward. Before Kanzaki's eyebrow could twitch, he exploded into a full step like a bullet.

"Whoaaahhh...aahhhhhh!!"

And then another step. If he couldn't run away from her, dodge to either side, or use anything as a shield, there was only one option left—to create a path for himself by pushing forward.

"I do not know what drives you to go this far, but..."

Kanzaki heaved a sigh tinged with a hint of sadness rather than shock, and...

Seven Glints.

Then shattered asphalt and shrapnel from trees swept over him like a cloud of dust.

"Ahh... ooohhh!!"

If he touched it with his right hand, he could erase it... Even if his brain understood that, though, his body opted not to take the risk. He threw his head forward and crouched. The seven-pronged onslaught whipping overhead made his heart stop.

He had no strategy or hope of winning. He'd only dodged it because he got a little lucky.

He took one more step forward—the third of four—with full force.

However enigmatic the Seven Glints attack was, it was fundamentally an *iai* strike, an ancient slashing technique in which the user unsheathes his or her sword, strikes, and then quickly resheathes it. A one-hit, certain-death attack. However, this meant that while the blade was free, its user was nothing more than a defenseless corpse.

If I can get close enough with the next step... I can win.

Kamijou's sliver of wiggle room was eradicated by the quiet *ching* of the sword reuniting with its sheath.

Then the tiny, incredibly fast sound of the sheathed blade.

Seven Glints.

Roar! At point-blank range...

The seven strikes stabbed directly for Kamijou's eyes before his reflexes to dodge could kick in.

"Damn it... ahhhhhhhhh!!"

Rather than advancing his attack or backpedaling as if to catch a ball aimed at his face, he stuck out his right fist in the path of the oncoming blade.

Kamijou's right hand could short out all preternatural phenomena, be they the powers of a vampire or even God.

The seven strikes seemed to all be bundled into a single blade this time, perhaps because he was so close. They rocketed toward him. Kamijou would blow the lot of them at once if he could just land a light touch with his Imagine Breaker.

The katanas, shining blue under the moonlight, gently caressed the skin on Kamijou's fingers…

…and **continued to sink in.**

"Wha—?!"

They didn't disappear. Even though he was using the Imagine Breaker, the absurd blades didn't disappear.

He immediately tried to pull his hand back, but it was too late. After all, he'd already used his bare hand as a shield against a katana. The blade had already made contact with his right hand.

Kanzaki looked at him and narrowed her eyes slightly.

The next moment, a watery, sopping noise of flesh being sliced open resonated in the area.

Cradling his blood-soaked right hand with his left, Kamijou crumpled to his knees on the spot.

Surprisingly enough, his five fingers hadn't been dismembered. They were all still attached.

Of course, that wasn't because Kamijou's fingers were unusually strong or because his assailant's skill had dulled. The fact that he hadn't had part of his body severed was simply *another* mercy Kanzaki had granted him. That was all.

Kneeling, he looked up.

Kanzaki's eyes were fixed on the perfectly circular blue moon, in front of which Kamijou could make out something like a red thread.

It looked like the silk of a spider's web, a spider's web drenched with fresh blood instead of dew. At last, he could see them: seven metal wires.

"I don't…believe it…" He bit down. "…You were never a sorcerer in the first place…were you?"

Her absurdly long sword was nothing but decoration.

Of *course*, he hadn't seen the moment she drew her sword. Kanzaki had never drawn it in the first place. She'd only slightly shifted the blade inside its sheath, then let it resettle. The movement obfuscated her hand while she manipulated the seven metal wires.

Kamijou's hand had only been spared because she'd loosened the cords just before his fingers were lopped off.

"I already said this. I heard about you from Stiyl," said Kanzaki, bored. "Do you understand now? This isn't a question of brute strength but finesse. Take rock-paper-scissors, for example. If you were to use rock for a hundred years, it wouldn't beat my paper in a thousand."

"..."

Kamijou clenched his blood-soaked fist.

"You seem to misapprehend something." Kanzaki regarded him now, her eyes full of pity. "I am not faking my true power with a cheap trick. The Seven Heavens Sword is no decoration. Even if you managed to pierce the Seven Glints, all that awaits you is the genuine Single Glint."

"..."

He clenched...his blood-soaked fist.

"Moreover...I have not even given my magic name."

"..."

...He clenched it.

"Please do not force me to say my name, young man." Kanzaki bit her lip. "I don't want to use that name ever again."

Kamijou's straining fist shuddered. This lady was clearly different from Stiyl. She was no one-trick pony. At the most basic level, the most fundamental level, the very ground level, she was made up of something completely different from Kamijou.

"...Like I would...surrender." However, he didn't relax his grip. He continued squeezing the hand he could no longer feel.

Index hadn't surrendered. She'd taken that gash in the back to save Kamijou.

"What was that?...I didn't hear you."

"I'm saying to shut the hell up, you stupid robot!!"

Kamijou tried throwing his bloodstained fist into the face of the woman standing over him.

But before he could, the tip of Kanzaki's boot jabbed his solar plexus. The air in his lungs spilled out in a rush, and at the same time, the black sheath of the Seven Heavens Sword came down against the side of his head like a baseball bat, knocking him off his feet. His body whirled like a dervish, and he landed on the ground on his shoulder.

Before he could cry out in pain, he spotted the sole of the boot attempting to crush his head.

He immediately rolled aside to dodge, but…

"Seven Glints."

With the voice came the seven strikes that pulverized the asphalt around him into dust. The explosion rained shrapnel down on him like bullets, pelting his entire body in a vicious downpour.

"Gh…agh…?!"

The pain was equivalent to having five or six people ganging up on him at once, and Kamijou writhed. Seeing him like this, Kanzaki drew closer, stomping the ground with the soles of her boots.

"Is that enough?" she asked, her tone soft and rather distressed. "There's no reason for you to go this far for her. Managing to survive more than thirty seconds against one of the top ten sorcerers in London is amazing. Having done this much, she won't blame you for it at all."

"…"

With what remained of his hazy consciousness, he thought back.

She was right. Index wouldn't blame him for anything.

But still, thought Kamijou.

It was for that very reason—because she continued to endure everything by herself, never blaming anyone—that Kamijou didn't want to give up.

He wanted to save her, the girl who smiled perfectly despite her suffering.

Looking as if he were an insect on its last legs, he compelled his right hand into a fist once more.

His body was still willing to move for him.

It was still moving.

"...Wh-why?" Kamijou sputtered, still curled up on the ground.

"You...seem awfully bored. You're...different from that Stiyl guy. You're...hesitating to finish off an enemy. If you really wanted to, you could have killed me for sure, but you **couldn't**... You've still got enough humanity left in you **to hesitate**, don't you?"

Kanzaki had told him over and over.

She wanted to end this before she was forced to give her magic name.

The rune sorcerer called Stiyl Magnus hadn't demonstrated even a fraction of a second's hesitation to do so.

"..."

Kanzaki fell silent. Kamijou didn't notice, given that he was about to pass out from the extreme pain.

"Then you get it, don't you? You all ganged up on her, ran her down until she collapsed from hunger; you carved open her back with a sword... You get that it's *wrong*, don't you?"

Kanzaki could do nothing but listen to the words spewing from his lips as if he were vomiting blood.

"Do you even know?! She doesn't have any memory of her life from before a year ago because of you. What in the world did you do to her to make her life this horrible?"

He didn't get an answer.

Kamijou didn't understand. Had it been for the sake of an incurably sick child or for a loved one who'd died...If they were targeting Index for some sort of "hope," if they wanted to obtain the 103,000 grimoires and upend the order of the world and become a demon god for that, then he could understand.

But this woman was different.

This person was part of an organization. She was told to do this. It was her job to do this. She was ordered to do this. It was asinine that she could hunt down a little girl and stab her in the back for such simplistic reasons.

"Wh...y?" Kamijou asked again through gritted teeth. "I'm a loser. Here I am, putting my life on the line, fighting like I'm about to die...

but I can't even protect a single girl. I'm a weakling who can't do anything but watch you take her away while I grovel."

Like he was about to cry, like a child.

"But you're different, aren't you?"

He didn't know what he was saying.

"With that much strength, you could protect anyone and anything; you could save anyone from anything..."

He didn't even know who he was talking to.

"...Why the hell are you doing something like this?"

He said it.

He was frustrated.

If he'd had that much strength, he could protect anything he wanted to, until the end.

He was frustrated.

This person was so overwhelmingly powerful, yet she squandered her strength with nothing better to do than follow around a little girl.

That was frustrating.

Because it was as if he was even lower than that.

It was so frustrating that he thought he was going to cry.

"..."

Silence piled upon silence.

Had Kamijou been fully conscious, he would certainly have been surprised.

"...It's not like I..."

The one who'd been cornered was Kanzaki.

With just Kamijou's words, one of the top ten sorcerers in London had been ensnared.

"It's not like I actually planned on cutting her...I thought the barrier on her habit, the Walking Church, was still working, so... I thought it would be absolutely harmless, so I just slashed a bit, but..."

He couldn't wrap his brain around Kanzaki's words.

"It's not like I'm doing this because I want to."

She went on.

"But if I don't do this, she can't keep living... She'll... Otherwise, she'll die."

Kaori Kanzaki spoke as if she were a child on the verge of tears.

"The name of the organization I belong to is the same as hers... Necessarius, of the Church of England." She spat out the words as if she was coughing up blood.

"She's my colleague... and a dear and important friend."

CHAPTER 3

The Grimoire Smiles Quietly

"Forget_me_not."

1

Kamijou didn't understand what she meant. He didn't understand the words coming out of her mouth.

Collapsed on the street, covered in blood, he looked up at Kanzaki and thought everything she'd said had been a hallucination induced by pain, because it was ridiculous. Index was being hunted by sorcerers and fleeing to the Church of England. There was no way the sorcerers chasing her were part of the Church of England, too.

"Have you ever heard of perfect recall?"

Kaori Kanzaki posed the question to him. Her voice was weak, her posture pained, and she certainly didn't look like one of the top ten sorcerers, even of London. She didn't look like anything but an exhausted, normal girl.

"Yeah... that's how she got the 103,000 books... right?" Kamijou managed through cut lips. "... She's got them all... in her head, she said. I didn't believe her... or in an ability that would let somebody memorize everything just by seeing it once. Because she's so... stupid. She definitely doesn't seem like... that sort of genius."

"... And how do you see her?"

"Just a girl."

Kanzaki wasn't surprised. Her expression grew fatigued, and she sighed.

"Do you think just an ordinary girl could have managed to evade us for an entire year?"

"..."

"Stiyl's flames, my Seven Glints and Single Glint...She couldn't have run away from sorcerers giving their magic names by herself without relying on magic like we do or on some kind of strange power like yours." Kanzaki smiled. "Just two members of the order were enough to make things turn out like this. If all of Necessarius was to become *my* enemy, I wouldn't last a month."

That's right.

Kamijou finally recognized Index's true strength. Even with his Imagine Breaker, an ability that could instantly nullify even miracles, he couldn't even evade the sorcerers for four days. But she had done it for...

"She is a bona fide genius," Kanzaki declared. "If she were mistreated, the devastation she could cause would be of the magnitude of natural disasters. The reason the Church doesn't treat her like an average person is obvious. It's because *everybody is scared*."

"...But still..." Kamijou bit down on his bloody lips. "...She's... human. She's not a tool...And her name...How can you forgive that...?!"

"You're right." Kanzaki nodded. "...On the one hand, her specs are no different from ordinary people like us."

"...?"

"More than eighty-five percent of her brain has been completely occupied by the 103,000-volume index...In her condition, completely weighted down and forced to function off the remaining fifteen percent, she's just like us."

That was a fascinating thought, but there was something else he wanted to know instead.

"...So...what? What the hell are you all doing? Isn't Necessarius the church Index belongs to? Why is the Church of Necessary Evils chasing her around? Why did Index call you evil sorcerers from a sorcerers' society?" He clenched his teeth for a moment. "Or what? Are you trying to say she's been lying to me?"

He couldn't believe that. If she'd just been trying to use him to her own ends, there would have been no reason for her to endanger and take a blow to the back to save him.

And logic aside, he didn't *want* to believe it.

Kaori Kanzaki hesitated briefly before answering, "...She wasn't lying to you."

She spoke as if the words were stuck in her throat, as if her heart was on the verge of being crushed.

"She doesn't remember anything."

"She doesn't know that we're both affiliated with Necessarius or why she's really being followed. She doesn't remember, so she was forced to make assumptions based on whatever information she had left. She figured it was probable that she was being targeted by a magical society bent on getting its hands on the 103,000 books."

Kamijou thought back.

Index had told him she didn't have any memories before one year ago.

"But...wait, just wait a second. Something's weird. Doesn't Index have perfect recall? How did she forget? And why did she lose her memories in the first place?"

"She didn't lose them." Kanzaki held her breath. "It would be more accurate to say that I erased them."

He didn't need to ask her how.

"*...Please do not force me to say my name, young man.*

"*...I don't want to use that name ever again.*"

"...Why?" he insisted. "Why?! You were Index's friend! And it wasn't just Index who thought so, either; it's written all over your face! Index was a close friend to you! So why?!"

Kamijou remembered the smile Index had given him.

That was a smile to her sole connection in the world, inspired by loneliness.

"...There was...It was the only thing I could do."

"Why?!" Kamijou shouted, as if howling at the moon.

"Because if I don't, Index will die."

Kamijou's **breath ceased.** His sensation of the heat of the midsummer night vanished all at once. His senses began thinning, as if he was trying to escape reality.

As if...as if he had become a corpse.

"I already told you that eighty-five percent of her brain is occupied storing the 103,000 books," Kanzaki said, her shoulders trembling. "That means she can only utilize the same fifteen percent as everyone else now. If she goes on creating memories like a regular person, her brain will blow out like a tire in no time."

"Th-that's..."

No. With no logic or reason to justify his reaction, he nevertheless raced to denial.

"But...But that's not right. You said she's just like us with the fifteen percent..."

"Yes. However, Index has something we do not: perfect recall." The emotion was steadily draining from Kanzaki's voice. "Let's start with, what exactly *is* perfect recall?"

"...The ability...to never forget something once you've seen it, right?"

"Then is the act of forgetting really such a bad thing?"

"..."

"The amount of free space in a human brain is actually a lot smaller than you might think. If you lived for a hundred years, the only reason you'd be capable of doing so is because your brain maintains itself, purging itself of unneeded memories...You can't remember what you ate for dinner a week ago, can you? Everyone's mind cleans itself up unconsciously. If it didn't, we wouldn't be able to carry on living.

"However," she continued haltingly.

"She cannot do that."

"..."

"From the number of leaves on every tree lining every street to each face comprising a crowd during rush hour to the shape of every single raindrop falling from the sky... Her brain is incapable of forgetting any of these, so it filled up with useless detritus almost immediately," she said icily. "... For Index, unable to utilize anything but that last fifteen percent in the first place, it's fatal. To survive, someone like her has no alternative but to borrow somebody's power to *make* her forget."

Kamijou's mind collapsed.

... This... What kind of fairy tale is this? An unlucky girl is hunted by evil magic users only to be saved by some boring guy. They become friends, and in the end, he sees her off, nursing a melancholy tightness in his chest... Wasn't that supposed to be the story here?

"... So before those who can use it take her away, we came to secure her."

"... I would like to secure the girl before I have to give my magic name."

"... How long...?"

Kamijou put the burning question out there. The moment he asked, he'd accepted her story as truth.

"How much longer can her brain hold until it blows out?"

"Erasure of her memories is conducted at exact one-year intervals," Kanzaki replied tiredly. "... She has three days left. If we do it too early or too late, it will be over. **We can only erase her memories at that precise time**... I hope that she hasn't been dealing with the migraines that appear and precede the end."

Kamijou shuddered. Index had certainly said she didn't have any memories from before a year ago.

And migraines... Since she was the only one who knew anything about sorcery, he'd taken her at her word when she said her collapse was a reaction from the healing magic.

But what if Index had been mistaken?

What if she was just on the brink, her overwrought brain poised to give out at any moment?

"Do you understand now?"

Kaori Kanzaki asked the question flatly. There were no tears in her eyes. She probably wouldn't have allowed herself such a cheap display of emotion.

"We have no intention of harming her. In fact, without us, she cannot be saved. Will you please hand her over before I have to give my magic name?"

"..."

Kamijou pictured Index's face before his eyes. He shut them tight and gritted his teeth again.

"You should know that she will not remember you after we erase her memories. You can tell from that piercing stare she gives us, can't you? However much you may care for her, once she wakes up, she will see you as nothing more than a natural predator stalking her 103,000 books."

"..." Kamijou suddenly felt as if something was out of place.

"Saving her will avail you nothing."

"...What did you say?"

The sentiment blossomed in his mind, as if it were gasoline suddenly ignited.

"What did you say?! Don't screw with me! It doesn't matter one bit whether or not she remembers! It looks like you don't get it, so I'll spell it out for you. I'm Index's friend and ally. And that's what I'm gonna stay, no matter what! That's the reality, whether it's written in that stupid holy book you all seem to love or not!!"

"..."

"I thought it was weird, you know? She forgets, but you can't just explain everything to her after the fact? Why the hell did you leave her like this? Why are you chasing her around like she's your enemy?! Why did you abandon her?! Why didn't you think about her feeli—"

"Shut the fuck up! You don't know a goddamn thing!"

* * *

Kanzaki's roar above him completely took the wind out of his tirade. Her raw emotion, no longer concerned with polite consideration of her words, squeezed Kamijou's heart.

"Don't act like you know!! How the hell do you think *we* feel, having to steal her memories like this?! Who the hell do you think you are?! You called Stiyl a homicidal maniac! How did you think *he* felt having to look at the two of you?! How much was *he* suffering?! How much resolve did it take for him to face the two of you like he was the enemy?! Do you have even the remotest fucking conception of the toll it takes on him to pretend to be the bad guy for the sake of a cherished friend?!"

"Wha—?"

Before Kamijou could so much as raise his voice in surprise at this complete attitude change, the side of his body was caved in by a merciless kick that sent him flying through the air as if he were a soccer ball. He hit the pavement sharply, rolling a good two or three meters.

He could taste blood all the way from his stomach to his mouth.

He hadn't even had time to acclimate himself to this latest agony when Kanzaki leaped at him, her figure silhouetted against the moon.

It had to be some kind of joke. She propelled three meters into the air on her leg strength alone and—

"...?!"

Kamijou heard a *crunch*.

The flat end of the Seven Heavens Sword's sheath crushed his arm like the stiletto of a high-heeled shoe.

But he wasn't even allowed to cry out in pain.

Kanzaki's face hovered over him, looking wholly on the cusp of shedding bloody tears.

Kamijou was scared.

He wasn't scared of her Seven Glints, or her Single Glint, or the true power of one of the top ten sorcerers in London.

He was scared of the unbridled human emotion aimed directly at him.

"I did my best, too! I did my best! Spring, summer, fall, and winter! We documented everything! We poured our hearts into diaries and photo albums to create memories she couldn't forget!"

With the relentless speed and precision of a seeing machine's needle, she rained the point of her sheath down on him over and over again.

Arms, legs, gut, chest, face—the blunt instrument punished him brutally, crushing different parts one after the other.

"...But it was pointless."

Kamijou could actually hear her gritting her teeth.

Her hand stopped abruptly.

"Even if she read the diaries or looked at the photo albums...All she did was say, 'I'm sorry.' No matter how many times we started from scratch to create new memories for her, no matter how many times the cycle repeats itself...family, friends, loved ones, *everything*...just fades to nothing."

She was shaking terribly, as if unable to take another step.

"We can't...take it anymore. We can't stand seeing her smile anymore."

For someone with Index's disposition, being torn away from loved ones must have been more excruciating than death.

And she was caught in this endless, hellish loop, forced to swallow that pain over and over again.

Partings more painful than death, only to be succeeded by the same preordained misery. It was beyond tragic.

So Kanzaki and the others had decided that, rather than burden her with cruel reunions, they would mitigate the suffering of each separation as much as they could. If Index had no worthwhile memories in the first place, it wouldn't come as such a shock when she lost them. So they abandoned their friend, setting themselves up as her enemies.

They painted over Index's memories—everything she was—in black.

They tried to make her final moments—her personal hell—a little less painful.

"..."

Kamijou got the picture.

These guys are professional sorcerers. They make the impossible possible. As Index forfeited her memories again and again, they had unquestionably sought out other alternatives.

But they'd never been blessed with an answer. Not once.

And Index, the victim in all of this, would never have blamed Stiyl or Kanzaki.

She would suffer the burden alone as always, always with the same smile.

Always starting over at zero, with no one to blame but themselves, Kanzaki and her partner were ultimately doomed to go bad.

But that was...

"Screw...that..." Kamijou bit down on his back teeth. "That's just your stupid, selfish rationalization. You never thought about Index for a second! Don't make me laugh... Don't pawn off your own damn cowardice on her!!"

For an entire year, Index had fled without asking anyone for help.

He absolutely wouldn't accept their solution. He couldn't accept it. He didn't want to.

"Then, what...what other way was there?!"

Kanzaki tightened her grip on the Seven Heavens Sword's sheath, bringing it down on Kamijou's face as hard as she could.

He jerked his tattered right hand to intercept, barely managing to restrain the weapon before it struck home.

I'm not worried about this kind of sorcerer anymore.

My body moves.

It moves!

"If you were just a little stronger..." He gritted his teeth. "If you weren't frauds who could actually follow through with your own lies...if you were scared of her losing her memories...then you just needed to resolve to give her even better ones the next year...! If she knew how much happiness lay ahead of her, losing her memories wouldn't have to be so scary. No one would have to run away anymore! That's all you needed to do!!"

Despite his shattered shoulder, he willed his right hand to grab a firmer hold on the sheath. He used every shred of his strength to pull himself up, the effort merely pumping streams of blood through the fresh lacerations covering his body.

"Do you still...plan on fighting with those wounds?"

"...Shut...up..."

"What will you accomplish by fighting?" It was Kanzaki who seemed confused. "Even if you defeat me, the whole of Necessarius is at my back. I may be one of the top ten sorcerers in London, but there are still others above me...If you look at the whole Church, I'm merely a pawn they are comfortable exiling to the Far East."

Yeah, that was probably true.

If she and Stiyl were really Index's friends, they would have been opposed to the Church's treatment of her. The fact that they weren't doing it meant that they were ineffectual; there was just that much of a gap in strength.

"I'm telling you...to shut...the hell up!!"

But all that was irrelevant.

His body rattled. Even though he felt like he could keel over at any moment, he forced his body forward again and glared into Kanzaki's eyes.

Confronted with just that powerless stare, one of the ten top sorcerers in London retreated a step.

"That's got nothing to do with it! Are you protecting people just because you feel like your strength obligates you?!"

Kamijou trudged forward one step on ragged legs.

"That's not it, is it?! Don't fool yourself! You got that power because there was something *you* wanted to protect!"

With his threadbare left hand, he grabbed her neck.

"Why the hell did you want that power?"

With his shredded right hand, he made a bloody fist.

"Who the hell did you want to protect with those hands?!"

Kamijou shoved his sluggish fist into her face. There was no strength behind the blow, and on contact, his fist started spurting blood as if it were a crushed tomato.

Nevertheless, Kanzaki staggered backward as if dealt a decisive blow.

Her Seven Heavens Sword fell from her hand and clattered to the asphalt.

"What the hell are you doing here?!" He stood over the crumpled Kanzaki. "You have all that power; you have all that talent... so why can't you do anything...?"

Thc ground swayed before his eyes.

As soon as he noticed, Kamijou collapsed in a heap as if his battery had died.

Get... up... She's gonna... attack again...

His vision flooded with darkness.

He tried to force his body to respond, tried to prepare for Kanzaki's counterattack despite the massive blood loss that had rendered him virtually sightless, but all the strength he could muster was barely sufficient to wiggle a little finger.

But her counterattack didn't come.

It didn't come.

2

A parched throat and sweltering body woke Kamijou.

"Touma?"

Realizing he was in Miss Komoe's apartment, he saw Index peering at him. He'd been sleeping on a futon.

Surprisingly, bright sunlight streamed through the window. He remembered losing to Kanzaki that night and passing out. He hadn't known at the timc how it would turn out, but the next thing he knew, he was here.

All in all, he was rather incredulous about the whole thing and therefore wasn't able to be happy just for being alive.

He didn't see Miss Komoe. She was probably out somewhere.

He did see a bowl of porridge placed on the tea table next to Index. Inwardly, he apologized to Index that the next thought even occurred to him, but it didn't seem likely that a girl who'd gotten hung up on his balcony and introduced herself by pestering him for food could actually cook for herself. It made more sense to assume Miss Komoe had made it and left it there for him.

"Jeez, it's...like I'm a patient here." Kamijou tried to move his body. "Ow, ow, ow... What's going on? The sun's up, so night's over... What time is it?"

"It wasn't just one night," answered Index, sniffling a little.

"?" Kamijou cocked an eyebrow, and Index delivered the news quietly.

"Three days."

"Three... days... Wait, what?! Why was I asleep that long?!"

"I don't know! Don't ask me!!"

Her reaction was sudden and defensive.

It was as if she was venting her anger and frustration. The sudden outburst caught Kamijou off guard, and he lost his breath.

"I don't know, I don't know, I don't know! I really didn't know anything! I was so focused on getting away from that flame sorcerer who'd been outside your house that I didn't even stop to think that you might be fighting another one!"

The blade composed of her words wasn't pointed at Kamijou.

These wounds were self-inflicted. He started to feel overwhelmed and soon found himself unable to say anything.

"Touma, Komoe said she found you lying in the middle of the street, and she brought you back to the apartment all torn up. While she was helping you, I was just thinking about myself. I didn't know you were about to die, and since I got away from that stupid sorcerer, I got all happy!" She stopped there abruptly.

Pausing momentarily, she slowly drew her breath in as if to say something decisive.

"...I couldn't save you, Touma."

Index's small shoulders trembled. She stopped moving and bit her lower lip.

But even now, Index wasn't crying for her own sake.

Her outlook on life allowed no sympathy or sentimentality for herself. To someone who'd vowed never to shed tears out of self pity, Kamijou knew he could never say anything comforting.

So instead, he thought:

Three days.

If she'd wanted to kill him, Kanzaki could have dispatched him at her leisure. But wait...wasn't it odd that they hadn't shown up in all that time to collect Index?

Then why? he wondered silently. He had no idea what they were planning.

Besides, he had a nagging suspicion that there was some deeper significance behind the words *three days*. He felt as if bugs were silently crawling up his spine. Then it came back to him.

The time limit!

"? Touma, what's wrong?"

Kamijou gave a start, but Index just looked at him, confused. The fact that she remembered him meant that the sorcerers hadn't erased her memories yet. What's more, she didn't appear to be exhibiting any of the related symptoms.

He was relieved, but he also wanted to kill himself for having wasted the last three valuable days like this. But he decided to keep that to himself. He didn't want Index to know.

"...Damn it. My body won't move. What is this? Am I mummified or something?"

"Does it hurt?"

"Does it hurt? If it hurt *that* much, I'd be writhing around in pain right now. What's with all the bandages, anyway? Isn't this a bit much?"

"..."

Index didn't answer.

And then, as if she couldn't endure it anymore, she started crying again.

That cut Kamijou to the quick more than any yelling could have. That was when it finally occurred to him: **feeling no pain may have meant he was in far *worse* shape than he supposed.**

Miss Komoe can't use healing magic again. He was pretty sure that's what Index had told him. In RPGs, wounds were easily dealt with if you just had MP, but it seemed the real world wasn't that considerate.

Kamijou looked at his right hand.

His shattered, crippled right hand was wrapped up in bandages.

"Oh, right, espers who've undergone a Curriculum can't use magic, right? Man, what a pain in the ass."

"...Yeah. Normal people and espers have **different circuits**, so..." She seemed dissatisfied. "It looks like your wounds will heal just with the bandages for now, but...Your science is so inconvenient. Our magic is probably faster."

"Well, you're right about that...But no need for that magic crap; I'll be fine."

"...What?" Index pouted at Kamijou's condescension. "Touma, after all this, you *still* don't believe in magic, do you? You're like some clueless boy whose crush doesn't know he's alive! Stubborn!"

"That wasn't what I meant!" retorted Kamijou, burying the back of his head in his pillow. "...It's just that, if possible, I don't want to see that expression you get when you talk about magic."

Kamijou remembered Index's explanation of rune magic in the hallway of his dormitory. Her eyes had been as empty and mechanical as cogs ticking in a watch.

Her words had been more polite than a bus announcement and more lacking in humanity than an ATM.

A unique, singular entity: the library of grimoires, the Index Librorum Prohibitorum.

He still couldn't believe that the girl in front of him was that.

Or rather, he didn't *want* to believe it.

"? Touma, do you hate explanations?"

"Huh...? Wait, don't you remember? You were droning like some kind of ventriloquist's dummy about Stiyl's runes. Man, you definitely got my attention with that one."

"...Oh...I get it. I...I awakened again, huh?"

"Awakened?"

That made it sound like that marionette was the "real" her.

The implication being that the kind girl sitting next to him was the "fake."

"Yeah. But I think I don't want you to ask too much about my awakened state."

Before he could press her on why, Index went on.

"Saying stuff you don't remember is kinda like talking in your sleep, so it's a little embarrassing.

"And also"—she moved her lips again—"I'm scared of how it's like slowly turning into an emotionless machine."

She smiled.

The smile told everyone not to worry about her, despite the fact that she looked to be on the verge of collapse.

No machine could have made an expression like that.

Only a human being could have created that smile.

"...I'm sorry," Kamijou apologized automatically. He was embarrassed for thinking her anything less than human, if only for a moment.

"It's all right, dummy." Index smirked, and he couldn't tell if it was actually all right or not. "Want something to eat? There's a whole big meal ready for the sick patient. There's porridge, fruit, and candy."

"Okay, but how am I supposed to eat it with these hand—"

Before he could finish, he realized she had chopsticks clamped in her right fist.

"...Umm, Miss Index?"

"Yeah? No reason to be all shy now, silly. If I hadn't fed you like this for three days straight, you would have starved."

"...No, thanks. Please, oh Lord, I need a little bit of time to meditate."

"Why? Are you not hungry?" Index put down the chopsticks. "Then do you want me to wipe off the sweat for you?"

"..Excuse me?"

An indescribable sensation made his entire body itch.

What is this? What's this unprecedented bad omen? What on earth is this awful sense of unease? If I ever see a videotape of these three days, I feel like I'll explode and die out of sheer embarrassment...

"...Anyway, I know you have good intentions and all, nothing malicious, but could you go sit over there, Index?"

"?" She paused for a moment. "I'm already sitting."

"..."

Index, holding a towel, was surely guided by her purest motives, but when his brain added the word *innocent* to the equation, Kamijou couldn't help but feel a bit skeevy.

"What's the matter?"

"Uhh..." Kamijou, fumbling for words, immediately tried to derail her. "Well, I'm lying on this futon, looking up at your face, and..."

"Is that weird? I'm a nun, so the least I can do is care for a sick person."

It wasn't weird. Her unsullied white habit and motherly demeanor made her seem like she was *actually* (sorry to say, Index) a nun.

More than anything, though...

Her cheeks were pink from crying, and when she looked at him with tears in her eyes, it was kind of...

For some reason, saying it annoyed him beyond reasoning, so he didn't.

"No, no. I was just thinking about how your nose hair is silver, too."

"..."

Index's face freeze-dried instantly.

"Touma, Touma. What do you think I have in my hand?"

"What do I...It's porridge, but...Hey, wait! Wait, don't let gravity—"

In a stroke of rotten luck, Kamijou's vision was unfortunately obscured in a flood of white by both the porridge and the bowl.

3

Kamijou, who now knew firsthand that rice porridge wasn't easily removed from futons or pajamas, and Index, who was slightly teary eyed and currently engaged in a fierce battle with the thick grains of rice, both heard a knock and looked at the door.

"Is it... Komoe?"

"... At least say you're sorry or something, idiot!"

Incidentally, even though the rice porridge was cool and hadn't scalded him, Kamijou had passed out for a few seconds in panicked convulsions at the moment the carbohydrates landed on him, due to his utter conviction that the gruel was actually very hot.

"Huh? What are you doing outside my house?" They heard the voice on the opposite side of the door. It was Miss Komoe, who'd been out somewhere until now. She appeared to have run into the visitors who'd knocked.

"Kami, I don't know who they are, but you have guests."

The door opened with a loud *click*.

Kamijou quaked.

Behind Miss Komoe stood two familiar sorcerers.

They looked a tiny bit relieved to find Index sitting there normally.

He scowled suspiciously. His immediate assumption would have been that they were there to collect Index... but they could easily have done that anytime during the three days Kamijou was unconscious. Regardless of when their treatment was scheduled, there was no reason to leave her here. They could have just locked her up somewhere in the interim.

...So why have they come now?

He shuddered. He suddenly recalled the power of the magicians' flames and sword, and his muscles tensed.

On the other hand, his reason for fighting Stiyl and Kanzaki in the first place had become somewhat ambiguous. They weren't "evil magic society soldiers A and B" anymore, but rather "Index's friends from the Church arrived to assist her." He was worried about Index's well-being, too, after all. In the end, there was nothing left to do but cooperate and hand her over to the Church.

However, that was merely his perspective.

From the sorcerers' vantage point, cooperation with Kamijou was wholly unnecessary. It would be an entirely simple matter to decapitate him right now and take Index back home.

Stiyl seemed to revel in Kamijou's tense demeanor.

"Hmm. In that kinda shape, you can't get away easily, can you?"

Stiyl's thinly veiled threat finally clued Kamijou in to his enemies' intentions.

Index could evade the sorcerers on her own. She'd spent nearly a year giving the Church the slip all by her lonesome. She could easily slip away and hole herself up somewhere **if it was just her.**

It wasn't even a matter of days now before she hit her limit. If they seriously let her elude them again, then, well...she *had* ducked the Church for almost a year. Even if they locked her up somewhere, she might have escaped, and she could also break out during the ceremony.

However, that story changed if she was saddled with Kamijou.

That's why the sorcerers hadn't killed him. That's why they'd returned Index to his side: so that she would stand by him, thereby willingly binding herself with the shackles they had prepared.

They'd stained their souls just to make absolutely certain that Index was securely in their grasp.

"Go home, sorcerers!"

Index planted herself in the magicians' path—for Kamijou's sake and no one else's.

She stood there with her arms spread wide, as if hanging on a cross for her sins.

Exactly as her tormentors had intended.

They'd clipped her wings by caging her with the shackles called "Kamijou."

"..."

Stiyl and Kanzaki suddenly trembled.

They trembled as if **even though things had turned out as** they'd **plotted and predicted, still they couldn't stand it.**

Kamijou thought about what Index's expression must have looked like. As her back was to him at the moment, he could only imagine.

Whatever it was, the sorcerers stood there, rooted in place. Miss Komoe, who wasn't even getting the brunt of it, averted her eyes as waves of emotion washed over her.

He thought about what they must have been experiencing.

How it must have felt to be judged and found wanting in the eyes of someone you'd tried to protect to the point of committing murder.

"...Stop...Index, they're...they're not enemi—"

"Go home!!"

Index wasn't listening.

"Please...I...I'll go wherever you want...I'll do whatever you want; I don't care anymore, just please, I'm begging you..."

Beneath her pervasive hatred, her voice mingled with that of a crying girl, tears dripping down her face.

"I'm begging you, please don't hurt Touma anymore!"

How much...?

Just how much damage did that deal to the sorcerers, once irreplaceable "companions"?

For a moment—and only for a moment—the two magic users smiled extremely painfully. As if giving up on something.

And then their eyes glazed over as if a switch had been flipped.

Theirs were no longer the gazes one directs at a friend; they were the chilling glares of sorcerers.

The conviction that they would mitigate the pain of parting as much as possible, rather than grant the cruel happiness of fleeting reunions...

The feelings that had forced them to abandon their companion and become her enemy, precisely because she *was* a dear friend to them...

Bonds like that couldn't be broken.

If Kamijou didn't have the guts to speak his mind, he'd be able to do nothing but watch silently as the worst-case scenario unfolded.

"There are twelve hours and thirty-eight minutes remaining before the limit."

Stiyl made the declaration in his sorcerer's voice.

Index probably didn't understand what he meant by "limit."

"We wanted to come here to see how well our shackles performed, to see whether or not you'd run away. This went a bit beyond our expectations, though, eh? If you don't want us to take away that toy of yours, then you should give up on any bright ideas you have about escape. Got it?"

It had to be an act. In reality, he must have wanted to tearfully rejoice at the fact that Index was safe. He must have wanted to run his hands through her hair, to press his forehead to hers to feel her warmth. That's how precious a friend she was to him.

That he addressed her so harshly must have simply been an indication that he wanted to act out his role perfectly. How much inner strength must he have had to prevent himself from spreading his own arms and becoming Index's own shield? Kamijou didn't understand.

Index didn't answer.

The two sorcerers said no more, leaving the apartment without another word.

Why...?

Why did it have to turn out this way? he thought, biting down on his back teeth.

"It's all right...okay?"

Finally, Index lowered her arms and slowly turned to face Kamijou.

He couldn't help but shut his eyes. He couldn't bring himself to look at her.

He couldn't bring himself to bear witness to Index's face, disheveled, covered with tears and relief.

"If I make a deal with them..." He heard her voice in the darkness. "...Then your normal life won't be broken anymore. I won't let them set another foot in here, so it's okay."

"..." Kamijou couldn't answer. He could only think, in the darkness, with his eyes closed.

... *Can I really let her go? Let our time together go?*

4

Night fell.

Index lay flat on her face next to the futon, asleep. She had drifted off before the sun went down, and the lights in the apartment hadn't even been turned on.

Miss Komoe was apparently going to the baths, so they were the only ones in the room.

Apparently. Far from at his best, Kamijou had also been sleeping, and when he awoke, it was night. Miss Komoe's room had no clock, so he didn't know what time it was. When he remembered the time limit, he felt a chill.

Index had quickly passed out in exhaustion, maybe as a result of the cumulative stress of the past three days. With her mouth hanging half open, she reminded him of a baby worn out after nursing from its mother.

It seemed as if she'd already abandoned her original goal of making it to the Church of England. Maybe she didn't want to have to drag the battered Kamijou along.

Every once in a while, she'd say his name in her sleep, which was a little embarrassing.

He confronted some complex feelings when he looked at her kitten-like, defenseless face.

It didn't matter how hard she tried or how stubborn she was; in the end, everything would go according to the Church's designs. Whether she reached a church safely or was captured by sorcerers en route, she would be returned to Necessarius, and her memories would be erased.

Suddenly, the phone rang.

The phone in Miss Komoe's apartment was an antique black

rotary dial. Kamijou regarded it lazily as it made an alarming ringing noise.

Answering it was just common sense, but Kamijou wasn't sure it was okay to use Miss Komoe's phone when she wasn't around. He grabbed the handset anyway. Not because he wanted to pick up, but because he would have felt bad if it woke up Index.

"It's me. Do you understand?"

What he heard from the other end of the line was a woman's very proper voice. He could tell through the receiver that she was making an effort to speak quietly, as if whispering a secret.

"Kanzaki... what was your first name?"

"No. For our mutual well-being, we should not remember each other's names. Is the girl... Is Index there?"

"She's sleeping over there, but... Wait, how do you know this number in the first place?"

"The same way I knew the address. I just looked it up." Her tone was stiff and unyielding. "If she is not awake, then all the better. Please listen to what I have to say."

"?" Kamijou frowned suspiciously.

"... I touched on this before, but her time limit is at midnight tonight. As per proper procedure, we have created a schedule that will end everything at that time."

Kamijou's heart froze.

He already knew. He knew there was no other way to save Index. But with the end hovering before his eyes, he suddenly began to feel backed into a corner.

"But...," Kamijou started in a ragged voice. "Why would you... go through all this to tell me? Stop it... If you tell me all this, I'll have to try and stop you even if my life's on the line."

"..." The receiver fell silent.

It was by no means completely quiet; it was a very human hush, intermingled with the sound of quiet breathing.

"... Does that mean you do not require time to part with her?"

"Wha—"

"I will come out and say this. When we tried to erase her memory the first time, we were absorbed with trying to capture memories with her those last three days. On the final night, we clung to her and cried hideously. I think that you at least deserve to be given the same consideration."

"Don't…screw with…me…," Kamijou responded despite himself, practically crushing the phone in his grip. "All that means is that you're telling me to give up, right?! Aren't you just telling me to **abandon any right I have to put in the effort to fight it to the death?!"**

"…"

"Listen up, because there's something you don't quite get. I haven't given up yet. No, I'm not giving up no matter what! If I lose a hundred times, I'll stand back up a hundred times, and if I lose a thousand times, I'll crawl back to my feet a thousand times! That's all there is to it, so just watch me do what you guys couldn't!!"

"This is neither a dialogue nor a negotiation, just a **message** and warning. Regardless of what you may want, we *will* pick her up by the time limit. If you would still try to stop us, then we need only crush you."

The sorcerer's voice was as smooth as a bank clerk's.

"You may be attempting to appeal to what human kindness remains in me…But that is all the more reason for me to make this a strict demand." Her voice was as cold as a katana wielded in the night air. "Before we arrive, say your parting words and leave that place. Your role was to serve as her shackles. The destiny of a chain is to be cut loose once it has served its purpose."

The sorcerer's words weren't laden with simple hatred or derision.

It almost sounded as if she wanted to spare someone from getting hurt, should he put forward another futile effort.

"Bull…shit…" For some reason, that hit a nerve, and Kamijou swore into the receiver, snapping back at her.

"Every single one of you…You blame your weakness on other people. Aren't you sorcerers? Can't your magic make the impossible

possible?! Then what the hell is this mess? Is magic really that useless?! Can you really face Index and honestly claim that you've tried every single, solitary spell?!"

"**...I cannot do anything with magic.** I'm not proud of it, but I refuse to placate her with empty words." Kanzaki sounded as if she was seething through her teeth. "If there was a way, we would have found it long ago. No one would want to have to endure this...this cruel ultimatum."

"...What are you saying?"

"You cannot give up because you do not know the facts. I did not want to spend these last hours so fruitlessly, but **I can at least help you to sink into despair**." As if reading fluidly from the Bible, she continued, "Her perfect recall ability is neither a preternatural talent like yours, nor is it magical like mine; it is just how she is. It is no different than having bad eyesight or hay fever. **It is not something that can be broken like some kind of hex.**"

"..."

"We are sorcerers. We may dispel magic by using magic in an environment created by magic."

"So it's some kind of anti-occult defensive system made by a sorcery expert. How annoying. Couldn't you do something if you used Index's 103,000 grimoires?! For people preaching about how you could obtain the **power of God** from her, it's pretty damn stingy for you to say you can't heal a single brain!"

"You're referring to demon gods. The Church's number one fear is that the Index Librorum Prohibitorum could rebel against them. That's why they placed a collar on her that requires the Church's maintenance to wipe her memories every year. Do you think they would have left a means for her to remove her own collar?" Kanzaki asked quietly. "...Most likely, there is a bias in those 103,000 books. For example, she may be unable to access grimoires related to memory manipulation or something along those lines. It's only natural to infer that some sort of security system would be in place."

Those bastards, Kamijou swore to himself. "…You said that eighty percent of Index's head is eaten up by the knowledge from those 103,000 books, right?"

"Yes. More precisely, it is eighty-five percent, but for us sorcerers, eradicating those 103,000 books is impossible. Not even an Inquisitor is capable of destroying a grimoire's original text. We couldn't expand the free space in her head without hollowing out the other fifteen percent: her memories."

"…Then what about *us* from the science world?"

"…" The other end of the receiver fell silent again.

Kamijou considered the possibility. He thought that if sorcerers had attacked the problem from all sides using their own field—magic—and it still wasn't effective, then what if they didn't give up but instead turned to a new field? Wouldn't that be the logical course of action?

For example, if that field was science…

They would certainly need somebody to chart their course. It would be comparable to hiring a translator in a foreign land so you could interact with the locals.

However, Kanzaki's next words caught him off guard.

"…Yes, there was a time we considered it," she explained. "To be honest, I'm not sure what should be done now. I had faith in the absolute power of magic, but it can't even save one girl. We have no choice but to grasp at straws at this point. I understand that, but…"

"…" He could guess what came next.

"…To be honest, I am hesitant to hand over a dear friend to science."

Even though he knew, her position when articulated stabbed at his brain.

"Part of me thinks that there is no way your science can accomplish what our magic cannot. Flooding her body with strange medicines and cutting her open with a knife…Such barbaric tactics would only serve to unnecessarily compromise her life span. **I don't want to see her violated by a machine.**"

"That's just... How can you say that when you haven't even tried? If that's the case, I have one question for you. You keep talking simply about killing memories, but do you even know what amnesia is in the first place?"

She had no answer.

As he suspected, she didn't know much about neuroscience. Kamijou dragged a Curriculum textbook on the floor to him with his feet. It was a Development recipe with a sprinkling of neuroscience, exceptional psychology, and reactionary pharmacology.

"You keep talking about taking away her memories, and perfect recall, and stuff like that. But even though *amnesia* is a simple word, there's more than one kind." He flipped through the pages. "Aging... well, senility is one, as is blacking out from intoxication. There's an illness called Alzheimer's, and TIA... where blood stops flowing to your brain and your memory vanishes. Halothane, isoflurane, fentanyl, all the full-body anesthetics—and then there are side effects from medicines like barbituric acid derivatives and benzodiazepines that can make you lose your memory."

"??? Benzo... What?"

Kanzaki reeled in an uncharacteristically feeble voice, but Kamijou ignored her. He was under no obligation to politely explain every little thing to her.

"To put it simply, **there are plenty of ways to medically remove a person's memories.** Which means there are methods **you haven't tried to wash away those 103,000 grimoires**, moron."

Kanzaki's breath caught in surprise.

But these were all ways to damage your brain cells, as opposed to ways to get rid of your memories. Old people suffering from dementia lose their memory over time, but that doesn't free up space to remember new things.

However, he didn't dare say that. Call it a bluff, but first he had to find a way to deal with the memory purge the sorcerers were trying to force on her.

"And besides, this is Academy City, you know? There's plenty of espers who manipulate minds using techniques like psychometry and puppeteering, and furthermore, there are a ton of agencies researching it. It's too soon to give up hope. At Tokiwadai alone, there's apparently a Level Five esper who can steal a person's memories just by touching them."

If anything, *this* was actually the last ray of hope.

The other end of the line was mute.

Kamijou continued talking, beating down Kanzaki, who'd started exhibiting signs of doubt. "So, what will you do, sorcerer? Are you still going to get in people's way? Are you going to give up; take the easy, temporary way out; and keep weighing the lives of other human beings like coins on a scale?"

"...For arguments intended to sway an enemy, those were cheap," replied Kanzaki with a hint of self-deprecation. "On the other hand, **for now**, we have the faith and the results that have saved her life in the past. I cannot trust your gamble, because it has no proven track record. Do you not think your suggestion is reckless?"

Now it was Kamijou's turn to fall mum momentarily.

He tried to come up with some counterargument, but not a single thing came to him.

He had to give up.

"...I guess so. In the end, we couldn't come to an understanding."

He had no choice but to completely acknowledge her as his enemy, even though her circumstances were the same and she *could* have understood.

"So it seems. If people who want the same things became allies as a matter of course, the world would certainly be more peaceful than it is now."

Kamijou gripped the handset a little bit harder.

With his right hand, the one weapon said to be capable of erasing even miracles.

"...Then I'll **crush you, my old enemy."**

"It is clearer than fire what the outcome will be, given the difference in our abilities. Will you still call my bet?"

"Yeah. I'll even raise. I'm gonna draw you into an environment where I'll win for sure." He bared his canines at the receiver.

Stiyl hadn't been less powerful than him after all. He'd won because Stiyl fell victim to the sprinkler. The point being that there should always be a way to negate an opponent's advantages by approaching a fight from the right angle.

"I will tell you in advance: The next time that girl collapses, please consider it to be too late." Kanzaki's warning was as sharp as the tip of a knife. "In any event, we will descend on your location at midnight tonight. You have very little time left, but I look forward to a splendidly futile effort."

"I'll wipe that grin off your face, sorcerer. I'll save her and steal the spotlight from you completely."

"I cannot wait." She snorted, then hung up.

Kamijou quietly replaced the receiver and then looked up at the ceiling, as if he could see the moon in the night sky beyond it.

"Damn it!"

He brought his right fist down on the tatami floor vigorously, as if he was pummeling a pinned opponent. His wrecked right hand didn't hurt in the slightest. His mind was in such chaos that it completely ignored the pain.

He'd talked pretty big on the phone with the sorcerer, but Kamijou was neither a neurosurgeon nor a professor of cerebral physiology. Even if science *could* somehow do something, a high school kid like him wasn't coming up with any breakthroughs about the proper course of treatment.

But he couldn't quit now just because he was stuck.

An intense sense of panic and uneasiness settled over him, as if he'd been plopped down in the middle of a flat, endless desert and told to haul ass back to town on his own.

When the time limit came, the sorcerers would mercilessly exterminate Index's memories. They were probably already hiding outside the apartment, countermeasures already implemented should he try making a break for it.

He didn't understand why they didn't just attack now. Did they empathize with him? Was Index too fragile to move this close to the end? He didn't know, and he didn't care.

He looked at Index's round face as she slept peacefully on the tatami.

Then, with an "Okay!" he tried to kick his brain into gear.

Despite the fact that there were more than a thousand research agencies in Academy City, big and small, as a student, Kamijou had no connections or pull with any of them. He needed to try contacting Miss Komoe to ask her instead.

She might think it was hopeless with so little time remaining. Index's limit was swiftly approaching, but... Actually, he had a secret plan. Since Index's brain blew if she kept creating memories, if he could somehow keep her asleep, wouldn't that stop her from creating memories and give him more time?

When he thought about drugs that induced a deathlike paralysis, it reeked of silliness and sounded very *Romeo and Juliet*–esque. He didn't have to go that far, though. Some laughing gas—a full-body anesthetic used during surgery—would be more than sufficient to place her into a deep sleep.

He also wasn't worried about the possibility of her dreams resulting in additional memory consumption. He'd learned a bit about sleep processes in his Development classes. The only time a person dreams is when he or she is in shallow slumber. A person entering deep sleep **would forget even having had dreams, and his or her mind would rest.**

Therefore, Kamijou needed two things.

First, he needed to ask for Miss Komoe to contact a neuroscience or mind ability–related research facility to help.

Second, he needed to evade the sorcerers' surveillance and get Index out of there, or else he needed to orchestrate a scenario where he could somehow defeat two magic users.

He started with calling Miss Komoe.

...At least, he was going to, but when he thought about it, he realized he didn't know her cell phone number.

"Ack, wow, I'm stupid...," he muttered to himself with half a mind to just curl up and die. He took a look around him.

The completely ordinary, cramped 4.5-tatami room suddenly struck him as a confusing labyrinth. The unlit room was as dark as the night sea, and even the small shadows from the piles of books and overturned beer cans seemed to be concealing things. He started getting a little queasy when he thought about how many drawers were in her dresser and cabinets.

He knew it was crazy to try and search everything for a cell number he didn't even know existed. He felt as if he'd been tasked to find a single battery someone had accidentally tossed into a garbage dump.

But he couldn't let that stop him. He decided to try looking for a number that might have been jotted down on a scrap of paper and started overturning things around him. Right now, every second was crucial, so looking for something he wasn't absolutely certain was there to be found was insane. With every heartbeat, his mind grew a little more frantic, and with every breath, impatience racked his brain. Someone peering through the window would no doubt have taken him for a punk trashing the place.

Reaching into the back of a cabinet drawer and pulling out a stack of books, he glanced at Index, still curled up and oblivious. For all of the madness surrounding the girl, time seemed frozen in the spot where she lay.

Seeing Index in full-on sleepy-cat mode while he busted his ass made him want to punch her in the face, but that didn't mean he missed the piece of paper that looked suspiciously accounting oriented that slipped out of a college-ruled notebook that he'd overturned.

It was a cell phone usage statement.

Kamijou scrambled to pick it up. There were eleven lines of numbers on it. Incidentally, he saw his teacher had a ridiculous 142,500-yen balance the previous month. Some telemarketers and scammers had probably locked her into conversations. Normally, he'd have spent a good three straight days rolling around on the floor laughing about this, but clearly this wasn't the time. *I need to call her*, he thought, heading for the black phone.

It seemed as if it took an eternity for him to identify the appropriate number.

From his warped sense of perspective, it could have been hours or minutes. His mind was backed so far into a corner that he'd lost any concept of time.

He dialed the number. As if rehearsed beforehand, Miss Komoe picked up after the third ring.

Kamijou, nearly foaming at the mouth, vomited into the handset an explanation that was difficult even for him to follow, given that he hadn't fully processed it all yet.

"...Hmm? Teacher's specialty is pyrokinesis, so I don't have many mind-hound-related contacts. For now, you could probably use the Takizawa Agency or Toudai's University Hospital, but their facilities are second-rate. It would be safer to call an esper in the field. If I remember correctly, Miss Yotsuba from Judgment is a Level Four telepath and quite obliging."

Miss Komoe answered helpfully, despite him not explaining the details.

He seriously began thinking he should have just asked Miss Komoe in the first place.

"But Kami, even if the professors at the research labs are night owls, it would be pretty hard for a student to call them at this hour. Do you want me to arrange a lab for her?"

"Do I want... No, Miss Komoe, I'm sorry, but this is time critical. Can't you get them out of bed or something?"

"Well...," Miss Komoe considered. After an irritatingly long pause, she replied:

"I mean, it's almost midnight, you know?"

Huh? Kamijou froze.

There was no clock in the apartment. Even if there *were*, Kamijou wouldn't have had the courage to check it.

His gaze slowly, awkwardly dropped to Index's sleeping form.

She seemed peaceful enough, curled up on the tatami. But her outstretched limbs weren't moving. They didn't even twitch.

"... In ... dex?" he prompted hesitantly.

No reaction. As if wholly incapacitated by a fever, she didn't respond.

The receiver droned something incoherent.

But Kamijou dropped it before he could make it out. A dank, cold sweat suddenly broke out on his palms. He felt something ominous, as if a bowling ball had been deposited in the pit of his stomach.

Then, he heard the metallic sound of footsteps walking up the apartment complex hallway.

"*... In any event, we will descend on your location at midnight tonight. You have very little time left, but I look forward to a splendidly futile effort.*"

The door to the apartment burst open violently the instant the warning came back to him.

The blue moonlight trickled into the room, much like sunlight leaking through trees in a forest.

The two sorcerers were silhouetted in the doorframe, the perfectly round moon at their backs.

Just then, Japan's clocks struck midnight.

A certain girl's time was up.

In other words, it was over.

CHAPTER 4

The Exorcist Decides the Ending

(N)Ever_Say_Good-bye.

1

The two sorcerers stepped into the apartment, over the broken door, bathed in the moonlight behind them.

This time, even though Stiyl and Kanzaki were right there, Index didn't stand between them and Kamijou. This time, she didn't shout at them to go away. She was breathing shallowly, as if a slight wind could have robbed her of her breath entirely. Soaked in sweat, as if critically ill.

Kamijou's head ached.

A fierce throbbing, as if his skull might shatter at as minute a sound as snow falling.

"..."

Nothing passed between him and the sorcerers.

Stiyl entered with his shoes on and shoved the speechless Kamijou aside with one hand. He hadn't put much power into the gesture, but Kamijou still toppled over. All of his strength gone, he dropped onto his rear on the tatami.

Stiyl didn't devote so much as a glance to him.

Squatting beside the motionless, outstretched Index, he whispered something to her too quietly for Kamijou to make out.

His shoulders were trembling.

Then he raised his voice, robust with the outrage of a man who'd witnessed a loved one hurt before his eyes.

"Referring to Moon Child, the Book of Crowley. We shall utilize a method for capturing an angel, then create a chain of summoning, capturing, and employing a fairy."

Stiyl stood again, fully prepared.

He turned, and his expression was entirely devoid of compassion.

He wore only the face of a sorcerer who had sacrificed his humanity to save a single girl.

"...Kanzaki, help me. **We shall kill her memories.**"

Those words pricked the frailest area of Kamijou's heart.

"Ah..." He understood, though. He understood that there was no other means of saving Index but to perform this awful task.

And Kamijou had told Kanzaki before that if she really was acting solely out of friendship for Index, then she shouldn't hesitate to eradicate her memories. However many times she lost her history, if they gave her happier and more interesting experiences to enjoy the next year to the fullest, it wouldn't be as hard on her.

But that was...

Wasn't that just a **compromise they made after giving up on pursuing other options?**

"..." Unconsciously, Kamijou's hands had balled into fists, and he was clenching them so hard that he was on the verge of crushing his fingernails.

Are you okay with this? Are you just going to give up? Even though there are memory- and mind-related research facilities in Academy City, you're going to give up like this? Are you really okay with using this stupid, old-fashioned "magic" to kill the memories of the person most important to you, over and over again? Isn't this the cruelest solution? Isn't it the easiest?

No, fine.

I don't give a damn about logic anymore.

You, Touma Kamijou.

Can you stand it if Index's memories of the week you spent together were wiped clean as casually as deleting a game's save data?

"...Wa...it..." Touma Kamijou looked up.

All he wanted to do was take a stand against the sorcerers trying to save Index, straightforwardly and honestly.

"Wait, wait a minute! Just a little bit longer! I'll know in just a little bit! There are 2.3 million espers in Academy City. There are more than a thousand research agencies overseeing them all. Psychometry, brainwashing, telekinesis, materialization! There are tons of espers who control minds and labs developing them all over the place! If we ask one of them, you might not have to resort to using this terrible magic!"

"..." Stiyl Magnus didn't say a word.

But Kamijou continued shouting at the flame sorcerer.

"You don't want to do this, either. Deep down in your hearts, you're hoping that you find some other way! So just wait a little bit... I'll find a happy ending where everyone can laugh together! So just...!!"

"..." Stiyl Magnus still held his tongue.

Kamijou didn't know why he was going this far. He'd only met Index a week ago. He'd lived sixteen years without her, so shouldn't he be able to live a normal life even if she was gone?

He should have been able to, but he knew he wouldn't.

He didn't know why. He didn't even know if he *needed* to know why.

It just *hurt*.

He wouldn't hear her voice or see her smile, her gestures, or anything about her, ever again.

Her memories of the week they'd shared were going to be erased as easily as the push of a reset button.

The thought of it made the most important, kindest part of his soul ache.

"..." Silence held sway.

It was elevator silence. It wasn't that there was nothing to make a sound, but the people inside were dedicated to maintaining the saturninity. It was a bizarre hush punctuated only by breathing.

He looked up.

Petrified, he probed the sorcerers' faces.

"Are you finished, you self-righteous brat?"

That was it.

Those were the only words that Stiyl Magnus, the rune magician, spoke.

He had certainly heard Kamijou's pleas.

He absorbed every word, crushed them into bite-sized pieces, and scooped up the meaning and emotion they conveyed.

But he didn't move so much as an eyebrow.

The desperate entreaty didn't persuade him so much as a millimeter.

"Out of the way," commanded the flame mage.

Kamijou didn't know how to organize his expression, which facial muscles to activate.

Not wasting a breath, Stiyl said, "Look," and pointed at something.

Before Kamijou could redirect his attention, Stiyl viciously grabbed the boy's hair.

"Look!!"

Kamijou was incapable of forming words.

Index's face was before him. It looked as if she might stop breathing at any moment.

"Can you still say that after seeing her like this?" Stiyl's voice quavered. "Can you still say it when she's seconds away from death?! To someone in such pain that she can't open her eyes?! Can you still tell us to *wait* because there's *something you want to try*?!"

"..."

Index's fingers stirred. Either she was just barely lucid or doing it unconsciously, but she moved her leaden hands with all her might, reaching to touch Kamijou's face.

As if desperately trying to protect him—as if she knew the sorcerer had a fistful of his hair.

As if she was saying that her own pain didn't matter at all.

"If you can, then you aren't even human anymore! Even with her in this condition, you want to give her medicine you've never tried, let a doctor whose name you don't even know mess around with her body and make her dependent on drugs? No human being would even entertain ideas like that!" Stiyl's roar pierced Kamijou's eardrums and into his brain.

"Answer me, esper. Are you still human? Or are you a monster who's abandoned his humanity?!"

"..."

Kamijou couldn't answer.

Stiyl followed up, as if stabbing a blade into the heart of a corpse.

He reached into his pocket and produced a small necklace with a cross.

"...This tool is required for erasing her memories." He dangled the cross in front of Kamijou's face. "Obviously it's magical. If you touch it with your right hand, it should lose all its power, just like my Innocentius."

The cross swayed back and forth as if taunting Kamijou, reminding him of a cheap hypnosis pendulum.

"But can you destroy it, esper?"

Kamijou regarded Stiyl as if paralyzed.

"Look at her suffer like this. **Can you take this in your hands?!** If you believe in your power so much, then erase it! You're nothing but a freak of nature pretending to be a hero!"

Kamijou watched.

He studied the cross swaying before his eyes. He fixated on the contemptible, memory-eradicating relic.

As Stiyl said, if he took it, he would stop them from erasing Index's memories.

There was nothing difficult about it. He just had to reach out his hand a bit and lightly stroke it with his fingers.

That was all. That would be all it took.

Kamijou squeezed his right hand as tightly as a boulder…

But he couldn't do it.

This sorcery was the sole means of saving Index *for now*, safely and certainly.

He couldn't touch it. Not in front of a girl suffering like this, enduring it all.

There was no way he could.

"With the preparations, at a minimum…twelve fifteen AM. With the power of Leo, I'll wipe her memory."

Stiyl sounded almost bored as he looked at Kamijou.

Twelve fifteen AM…It probably wasn't even ten minutes until then.

"…!!"

Kamijou wanted to shout *Stop!* or to scream *Wait!* but he wouldn't be the one to suffer if he did. The price for his selfishness would be paid in full by Index.

Just accept it.

"My name? It's Index, okay?"

Just accept it already.

"And, um, if you gave me some food to fill up my tummy, Index would be happy!"

Touma Kamijou, just acknowledge that you have neither the power nor the right to save Index!

Kamijou couldn't call out.

He just bit down on his teeth, stared at the ceiling…and let a tear fall from his eye, unable to hold it back any longer.

"…Hey, sorcerer."

He spoke in a stupor, still looking up at the ceiling with his back against the bookshelf.

"What do you think my last words to her should be?"

"We have no time to spare for nonsense like that."

"I see," he replied in a daze.

Stiyl advanced on Kamijou again, the boy looking as if he'd stay rooted to that spot forever.

"Can you get out of here, you monster?" Stiyl sized him up. "...Your right hand canceled my flames. I still don't understand the principle behind it...but I don't want it screwing up what we're about to do."

"I see," he repeated, bewildered.

Kamijou chuckled quietly, as if taking his last breath.

"...It was the same when she got slashed in the back. I wonder why I can't do anything."

Don't ask me, said Stiyl's eyes.

"I have this awesome right hand that can even erase God's miracles." He spoke as if he was about to collapse. "...Why can't I save just one person...? Just one suffering girl?"

He was laughing.

He didn't curse fate, and he didn't blame his rotten luck. He just bit down in frustration at his own powerlessness.

Kanzaki averted her eyes painfully and then told him, "There are still about ten minutes left before we perform the ritual at twelve fifteen."

Stiyl stared at her as if she had three heads.

But Kanzaki met his eyes and smiled a little.

"...On the night we first promised to erase her memories, we cried all evening at her side. Isn't that right, Stiyl?"

"...Gh." Stiyl's words got caught in his throat. "W-we don't know what this guy's gonna do. What if he tries to kill her and then himself while we're not looking?"

"If he wanted to do that, wouldn't he have touched the cross? You used a real cross, rather than a fake one, because you knew he was still human, didn't you?"

"But..."

"Either way, we cannot perform the ritual until the proper time. If we leave him with regrets now, it opens us up to the possibility of his interference in the middle of the ritual, Stiyl."

Stiyl gritted his teeth.

He looked poised to rip out Kamijou's throat, as if he were some sort of wild beast. But he held back, saying:

"Ten minutes. Got it?!"

He promptly turned on his heel and headed for the door.

Kanzaki said nothing, but her eyes were smiling in a very painful sort of way as she followed her partner out.

The door closed.

Kamijou and Index were alone. He had risked *her* welfare—not his—to gain these ten minutes while her life slipped away. But he didn't know what he should do.

"Ah…ka, ha…"

As she lay there limply, a voice struggled to escape Index's mouth, making Kamijou's shoulders suddenly quiver.

She had opened her eyes a little bit, and her sole concern seemed to be why she was on the futon and where he had gone.

Once again, she disregarded her own welfare entirely.

"…"

Kamijou gritted his teeth again. Facing her was more terrifying than fighting sorcerers.

But he couldn't bring himself to run away.

"Tou…ma?"

Kamijou approached the futon, and Index, with her sweat-covered face, looked relieved from the bottom of her heart.

"…I'm sorry."

He apologized at her side, looking down into her eyes.

"…? Touma…There's some kind of magic circle in here…"

Having been unconscious until now, Index didn't realize the circle had been drawn by the two sorcerers. She looked at the pattern on the wall near the futon and tilted her head in confusion, looking every bit a little girl.

"…"

For a moment, Kamijou clenched his teeth again.

But only for a moment. Before anyone would have been able to notice, his expression softened.

"...They said it's healing magic. We can't have you suffering with that terrible headache, can we?"

"? Magic... Whose?"

No sooner had she posed the question than Index finally realized the possibility.

"?!"

She forced her inert body to move and tried springing to her feet. The instant he saw the distorted look of pain that shot across her face, Kamijou took Index by the shoulders and forced her back down onto the futon.

"Touma! Those sorcerers came again, didn't they?! Touma, you've gotta get out of here!"

Index looked at him incredulously. She knew just how dangerous sorcerers were and worried for Kamijou with every fiber of her being.

"...It's all right, Index."

"Touma!"

"It's over... It's all over."

"Touma," she muttered quietly, the strength draining from her body.

Kamijou didn't know what sort of aspect his face had taken on.

"...I'm sorry," he said. "I'll get strong. I won't lose ever again. I'll get strong enough to blow away all these people treating you like crap, I promise..."

Crying would be cowardly.

Inviting her sympathy would be unpardonable.

"...Just you wait. Next time, I'll save you for sure, all right?"

How did his face look in Index's eyes?

How did his voice sound to Index's ears?

"Okay. I'll be waiting."

She didn't know the situation, so it must have looked as if Kamijou had sold her out to save himself after losing to the sorcerers.

But she still smiled.

It was a weak smile, a perfect smile, and a smile that could disintegrate at any moment.

Kamijou didn't understand.

He no longer understood how she was capable of placing so much trust in someone.

But it was enough for him to make up his mind.

He told her that once her headache healed, they'd beat them and win their freedom.

He told her he wanted to go somewhere with her, like the beach, but that they'd do that after his makeup classes ended.

He asked her if she might want to transfer into his school after vacation ended.

Index said that she wanted to make lots of memories.

Kamijou promised that they definitely would.

He went through with the lie.

He no longer cared what was right and what was wrong. He didn't need cheap morality if it was cold and unkind to her. If it couldn't ease one girl's suffering.

The name Touma Kamijou didn't need to be labeled good or evil.

The stamp of a fraud was more than enough.

Thus, he didn't shed a single tear.

Not even one.

"..."

The strength in Index's hand failed, and it fell to the futon with a little *thump*.

Index, once more unconscious, looked like a corpse.

"But..."

Her countenance gave the impression that she was enduring a feverish nightmare. Kamijou bit his lip softly.

"...This ending is just unacceptable."

He tasted blood where his teeth sank into his skin.

He was mortified by his helplessness, despite the fact that any action he might have taken would have been a mistake. Kamijou could do nothing. He couldn't do anything about the knowledge of the 103,000 grimoires consuming 85 percent of Index's brain, and he couldn't safeguard the memories stored in the remaining 15 percent.

"...Huh?"

Having surrendered his thoughts to despair, he suddenly got the sense that something didn't add up.

Eighty-five percent?

Creak.

He looked down, contemplating Index's feverish face.

Eighty-five percent. Yes, Kanzaki had said so, hadn't she? Eighty-five percent of Index's mind was devoted to storage of the 103,000 grimoires. So her brain was compressed, and the remaining 15 percent could store no more than a year's worth of experiences. If she absorbed any more memory than that, her brain would overload.

But wait.

Why was it that 15 percent of her brain was incapable of retaining more than a year's worth of memory?

He didn't know how unique perfect recall was. But he didn't think it was so rare that Index would have been the only person in the world to have it.

And other people with perfect recall didn't require having *their* memories wiped with some ridiculous sorcery.

But if Kanzaki still maintained that 15 percent of her brain was only capable of storing a year's worth of memories, then...

"...Wouldn't **those people die when they turned six or seven...?**"

If Index's "disease" was so terminal, wouldn't it be a lot more famous?

Even more than that, though...

Where did Kanzaki even get that 85 percent figure?

Who exactly had given her the information?

And...

* * *

Most importantly, was that 85 percent even *correct*?

"... They got us."

What if, hypothetically, Kanzaki didn't know anything about neuroscience? What if she was just being fed information like that by her superiors—by the Church?

Kamijou started getting an extremely bad feeling about the whole setup.

He immediately dove for the black telephone in the corner of the room. Miss Komoe was out somewhere again. He had no problem finding her cell number, having just made a mess of the entire room to locate it.

The mechanical ringing sound irritated him as he waited for his teacher to pick up.

Kanzaki's explanation of Index's perfect recall ability had to be off somehow. And what if the Church had planted that mistake? Maybe there was a secret buried there.

The phone connected with a staticky *click*.

"Teacher!!" he shouted into the phone automatically.

"Yeah~ That's Kami, isn't it~ You really shouldn't use Teacher's phone whenever you want like this~"

"... Um, you sound like you're having a good time."

"Yeah~ Teacher is at the bathhouse right now! I'm test-driving a new massage chair~ I've got a coffee milk in one hand~ Ahh~"

"..."

He considered pulverizing the receiver in his hand, but Index took priority.

"Teacher. Please, listen to me..."

Kamijou asked about perfect recall.

What was it like? Does capturing a year's worth of memories really use up 15 percent of your brain? In other words, was it a lethal trait that only permitted a six- or seven-year life span?

"Of course not~" Miss Komoe cut him off. "Yes, the perfect recall ability necessitates the retention of useless information—like sales in last year's supermarket circulars—but~ **There's no way that will blow out your brain or anything~** People with the ability will just carry hundreds of years' worth of memories with them to the grave, that's all. **Human brains are capable of remembering about a hundred and forty years of data, after all~"**

Kamijou's heart almost beat out of his chest.

"B-but what if, hypothetically, somebody used it to memorize a crazy amount of stuff? Like if you read all the books in a library... would your brain fry then?"

"Huh...Kamijou, you really are flunking your Development courses~" Komoe observed merrily. "Listen, Kami. In the first place, a person's memory isn't actually one thing. There are lots of different kinds~ Semantic memory governs language and knowledge, procedural memory governs how we get used to certain movements, and episodic memory governs actual memories of events~ There are tons~"

"Umm, Teacher...I don't exactly understand what you're saying."

"In other words...," Miss Komoe continued, still using her happy, explanatory voice, "...different things are categorized into different types of memory~ Kind of like regular trash and recyclables, I guess? For example, even if you hit your head real hard and got amnesia, you wouldn't go back to babbling and crawling around like a baby, right~?"

"...So, that means..."

"Yes~ However much you put into your semantic memory by memorizing books, compressing your episodic memory **is a neurological impossibility~"**

The words hit him in the head like a ton of bricks.

The handset slipped out of his hand and fell, colliding with the cradle and cutting off their conversation, but Kamijou didn't have time to think about that.

The Church was lying to Kanzaki.

Index's perfect recall wasn't life threatening at all.

"But why...?" Kamijou muttered, dazed. Yes, why? Even if the Church hadn't done anything to her, why would they lie about Index when she was perfectly healthy, claiming she'd die unless she was treated annually?

And Index, plainly suffering before his eyes this very moment, certainly didn't look like she was faking it. If her perfect recall wasn't the problem, then what *was* the source of her affliction?

"...Ah."

Once he'd thought it through, Kamijou had to suppress the urge to burst out laughing.

I see. The Church wanted to put a collar on Index.

A collar forcing her to receive regular yearly maintenance from the Church or forfeit her life. A collar to ensure her loyalty, and thus the safety of the 103,000 grimoires.

What if Index's body had originally been totally fine, and she didn't need to undergo weird rituals and ceremonies?

What if Index was capable of surviving just fine on her own without any of the hokum or mumbo jumbo?

If that was the case, the Church would never let it stand. There was no telling where she might disappear to after memorizing the 103,000 grimoires. There was no way they *wouldn't* collar her.

He repeated it back to himself: The Church wanted to put a collar on Index.

The explanation, then, was simple.

The Church had rigged something in Index's head, which had been just fine in the first place.

"...Ha-ha."

Yup. It was akin to packing a ten-liter bucket with enough concrete so that you could only fill it with one liter of water.

They messed with Index's head and made it so that one year's worth of memories would burn out her brain.

They made certain she was dependent on the Church's rituals and procedures.

They forced her friends to swallow their tears and bend to the will of the Church.

...They'd scripted a demonic program that even accounted for human kindness and compassion.

"...But that doesn't matter."

No, none of it was of any consequence right now.

There was only one problem requiring immediate attention: figuring out what kind of security measures the Church had employed to make Index suffer like this. The same way that Academy City, which supervised Kamijou and the other espers, was on the cutting edge of science, Necessarius, which oversaw sorcerers, must have been on the cutting edge of *something*.

Yes. If the obstacle was an abnormal power like magic...

...then Touma Kamijou's right hand could obliterate even a miracle with a single touch.

Kamijou thought about the time in the clockless room.

There probably weren't even minutes remaining before the start of the ritual. Next, he looked at the apartment door. Would the sorcerers believe him if he explained this truth to them? The answer was no. He was just a high school student. He wasn't a licensed neurophysiologist, and moreover, when you got right down to it, the two parties were clearly at odds. He doubted they'd take him at his word.

His gaze fell.

He looked at Index, lying on the futon, her exhausted limbs outstretched. She was drenched head to toe with a repulsive sweat. Her silver hair looked as if it had been dipped in a bucket of water. Her face was flushed, and her eyebrows twitched periodically in pain, the way they might if she was hospitalized with a serious malady.

"Look at her. This suffering girl lying at your feet, can you take this into your hands?! If you believe in your power so much, then erase it! You're nothing but a freak of nature pretending to be a hero!"

Kamijou chuckled, recalling Stiyl's accusation, which had shattered his resolve just moments earlier.

The world had changed enough that he could laugh.

"I'm not pretending to be the hero…"

Grinning, he undid the white bandages wrapped snugly around his right hand, as if breaking a seal.

"…I will *become* the hero."

He said this, smiling, while pressing his tattered right hand to Index's forehead.

People said his right hand could eradicate miracles, but it couldn't take down a single delinquent, or raise his test scores, or make him popular with girls. He'd thought it completely useless.

But maybe there was just one thing it was good for.

If it allowed him to save this suffering girl, then Kamijou thought it was a marvelous ability.

…

…

…?

"…Huh, what?"

Nothing happened. Nothing at all.

There was no noise or light. Had he undone the spell placed on Index by the Church? No, she was still grimacing in pain. He got the impression that nothing had changed.

Kamijou tilted his head in puzzlement and tried touching her cheeks and the whorl of her hair, but still nothing happened. No change. No nothing…but that's when he remembered.

Kamijou had already touched Index a few times.

For example, after pummeling Stiyl at his dormitory, he'd been touching her when he carried her away, and he'd lightly flicked her forehead after she'd told him who she really was. Of course there was no sign of a change.

Kamijou twisted his head. He couldn't imagine that his supposition was mistaken. And there shouldn't have been any sort of "abnormal influence" that his right hand couldn't interrupt. So…

So…where hadn't he touched Index yet?

"……………………………………………………………………
…………………………………………………………Ah."

His mind almost leaped somewhere extremely erotic, but he steered his thoughts out of the gutter.

But the process of elimination told him there was nowhere else left. If some sort of enchantment had been placed on Index, and if his right hand could cancel out any magic, then he hadn't yet touched the point of enchantment.

But where was it?

Kamijou examined Index's inflamed face. *Memory-related magic... It would have to be applied to her head or somewhere close, right?* If there was a magic circle inside her spinal cord or something, then Kamijou couldn't do anything about it, of course. If it was inside her, his germ-filled hands could never touch—

"...Oh."

He looked at Index's face again.

Her painfully flinching eyebrows, her tightly squeezed eyes, her nose dripping sweat like mud...He ignored all those, focusing on the dainty lips exhaling shallow breaths.

He took the thumb and index finger of his right hand and slid them between those lips, forcing her mouth open.

The back of her throat.

That was where the brain lacked the skull's protection, and in a straight line, it was even closer to her brain than the whorl of her hair. People would rarely see and never touch it. In the back of the dark red throat, he saw a single, eerie mark carved in black. It looked like a symbol you might see on a televised horoscope program.

"..."

Kamijou squinted his eyes once, then prepared himself and stuck his hand into her mouth again.

His finger slid into her oral cavity, wriggling like a worm, as if it were a separate life-form. Abnormally hot saliva spilled over his digit. He hesitated at the uncanny sensation of her tongue, and then, as if to pierce her throat, jammed his finger all the way in.

Index's body shuddered with a violent gag reflex.

Click. A feeling somewhat similar to a static discharge shocked his right index finger.

Bang! Suddenly, Kamijou's right hand was flung forcefully backward.

"Gah…?!"

Globules of his own blood splattered the futon and tatami.

The shock left his wrist feeling as if a handgun had blasted it. He immediately inspected his right hand. The wound Kanzaki had originally dealt him had reopened, and fresh blood streamed with a *drip-drop* onto the tatami.

Looking beyond the hand he'd raised to his face, he saw…

Index, collapsed in exhaustion mere moments ago, lifted her eyelids delicately. A brilliant red glow.

This was not a natural eye color.

It was the illumination from two bloodred magic circles floating in her eyeballs.

Crap…!! An instinctive shiver ran down Kamijou's spine. He immediately tried thrusting his ruined right hand forward again.

Before he could, though, Index's eyes flared a brilliant crimson, and something exploded.

Crash!! A powerful impact tossed his body into the bookcase in front of him. The wooden shelves fractured all at once, and the sounds of falling books echoed through the room. Every single joint in his body exploded in searing pain.

Shaking terribly, he was barely able to stand again. His legs felt as if they were going to fall apart. His saliva had taken on the metallic tang of blood.

"…Warning. Reading from chapter three, verse two. Barriers one through three of the collar of Index Librorum Prohibitorum destroyed. Penetration of all barriers confirmed. Preparing for regeneration… Failed. Self-regeneration of the collar impossible. Now prioritizing interception of intruder to preserve the 103,000-volume library."

Kamijou watched the reaction unfolding before him.

As if she had no bones or joints, she rose lazily, her movements sluggish, as if she were composed of jelly packed into a bag. The crimson magic symbols inscribed on her irises pierced right through him.

They may have been eyeballs, but they definitely weren't human.

There was no humanity in them, and no feminine warmth.

Kamijou had seen these eyes once before. After she'd been slashed from behind by Kanzaki, Index, collapsed on the floor of his dormitory, had spoken to him mechanically, lecturing on the subject of runic magic.

I don't have any magical power, so I can't use magic.

"...Now that I think of it, there was one thing I never asked you."

Kamijou cradled his shredded right hand and mumbled quietly in his mouth.

"If you're not an esper, then why the hell don't you have any magical power?"

The reason was likely due to the Church having prepared a two- or three-layer security system inside her. If someone was to learn the truth behind her perfect recall ability and tried to unlock the collar, Index would automatically manipulate the 103,000 grimoires and tap the most powerful magic she could reference to stop them. Maybe an automatic interception system like that required all of her magical energies.

"...Using the 103,000-volume library to reverse engineer the magical technique that destroyed the barriers...Failed. No matching sorcery found. Exposing structure of the technique and setting up a Local Weapon for use against intruder."

Index twisted her small neck as if she were a corpse being manipulated by string.

"Success. Preparation of most efficient counter-magic against specific intruder complete. Invoking Local Weapon Saint George's Hallowed Ground and destroying intruder."

* * *

Grakk! There was a tremendous noise, and the sigils in Index's eyes expanded quickly. The two magic circles, now two meters in diameter, positioned themselves in front of Index's face, overlapping. They were fixed in front of each of her eyes; when Index moved her head slightly, they followed her motion.

"."

Index sang something incomprehensible to the human mind.

The two magic circles with Index's eyes as their anchors momentarily shone, then exploded. It was as if a single point in the air had detonated, that point being the middle of Index's forehead. It looked like a rupture of a high-tension current, which scattered lightning in all directions.

However, these weren't bluish-white sparks. This lightning was pitch-black.

It's silly to say something so unscientific, but the fissures honestly looked as if they were ripping through space itself. *Grakk!* Centered at the intersection of the two magic circles, the black fractures spread through the air as if it were glass that had been struck by a bullet, and they extended to the corners of the room. They formed a single rampart, as if preventing anyone or anything from approaching Index.

Then, the innards of the fissures started to swell and pulse, as if something was in there.

What emerged from the partially opened maw of the pitch-black ruptures was a scent reminiscent of a beast.

"Uh."

Kamijou suddenly realized something.

It was neither logic nor reason, neither far-fetched conjecture nor rationality. It was something more fundamental, something closer to instinct, that was screaming inside his mind. He didn't know exactly *what* was in those fissures. But he got the distinct feeling that just looking at it with his naked eye would eradicate his entire existence.

". Ha." Kamijou was trembling.

The fractures grew bigger and bigger and bigger, and he knew the thing inside was getting closer. But Kamijou couldn't move. He quaked and quavered and palpitated because…

Because if he defeated that…

…then he would have saved Index all by himself, with no one else's help.

"Aha-ha-ha-ha-ha-ha-ha-ha-ha-ha-ha-ha-ha-ha-ha-ha-ha-ha-ha-ha-ha-ha!!"

Kamijou was trembling with delight.

Scared? Why would I be? I've waited for this for so long. I've had this useless hand that can't take down delinquents, can't raise my test scores, and can't make me popular with girls.

But even so, when one girl's back got sliced open because of me… When I was told that I would interfere with the healing magic and ran out of the apartment… When I got beaten to a pulp by that wire-wielding samurai…! I cursed my powerlessness, but I still hoped and prayed I could save this one girl!

It's not like I wanted *to be the hero of a story.*

The power sleeping in my right hand can even erase the very story itself!

Just four meters.

I can end everything just by touching her one more time!

And so, Kamijou dashed toward the fissures—and toward Index, who waited behind them.

He clenched his right hand.

He did it to destroy the ending of this cruel story. The foolish, infinite loop.

At the same time, with another high-pitched shriek, the fissures expanded all at once and opened.

It had all the subtle nuance of slicing open a struggling virgin. From the inside, the giant fissures stretching from one corner of the room to another, *something* peeked out.

Accompanied by an ear-splitting roar, a pillar of light erupted from the Stygian depths.

It was analogous to a beam fired from a laser, about one meter in diameter. The moment the face-melting, white-hot light lanced at him, Kamijou didn't hesitate to raise his tattered right hand in front of his face.

There was a loud hissing sound reminiscent of flesh being pressed against a hot plate.

But it didn't hurt. It wasn't hot. The instant the pillar of light collided with his right hand, it scattered everywhere, as if it were a stream of water from a fire hose bouncing off an invisible wall.

However, Kamijou couldn't completely dispel the pillar of light itself.

Just like Stiyl's Witch-Hunter King, Innocentius, it felt as if no matter how much he erased, there was still more. His feet started to gradually slide backward across the tatami, and his right arm felt as if it might fly off his body from the pressure.

No... This isn't like... What?!

His right hand feeling a hair's breadth from dismemberment, Kamijou immediately braced it with his left, grabbing his right wrist. A shocking pain erupted on the palm of his right hand. **The magic was cutting into his skin...** His right hand's ability couldn't keep up, and the beam was edging closer to Kamijou, one millimeter at a time.

It's not just the sheer quantity...! It's like every single photon has its own properties!!

Maybe Index was using each of the 103,000 grimoires to cast 103,000 spells simultaneously. Each individual volume meant certain death, and she was using all of them at once.

He heard a clamor outside the door of the apartment.

The instant they finally figured out something was wrong, the two sorcerers threw open the door and dove into the room.

"Damn! What are you doing?! Why do you insist on this futile—"

He heard Stiyl shouting something at him, but in the middle of it, the sorcerer's breath caught in his throat as if he'd been punched in the back. His face drained of all color when he saw the pillar of light before his eyes and that it was Index who'd unleashed it.

For Kanzaki's part... Kanzaki, who'd seemed so aloof and powerful before, was dumbfounded at the sight.

"...D-dragon Breath...I don't believe it. How can she even use magic in the first place?!"

Kamijou didn't turn to look at them.

It wasn't really an option, and he didn't want to avert his eyes from reality—or Index—any longer.

"Hey, do you have any idea what this is?!" he shouted, staring straight ahead. "Its name? Its form?! Its weakness?! Explain every single detail to me right now!!"

"...But, well... What..."

"You're so aggravating! Can't you tell just by looking?! Index is using magic, so the Church has been *lying* to you and saying she can't!" Kamijou bickered while dispelling the energy spear. "Yeah, that's right! The whole 'erase Index's memory every year' thing was a big, fat lie, too! The Church's magic was what was compressing her mind, so if I wipe this thing out, there won't be any need to erase her memory anymore!!"

Kamijou's feet continued losing ground, little by little.

The pillar of light doubled its intensity, as if to tear off the toes he was digging into the tatami. It was a nightmare.

"Calm down! Think about it logically! Do you really think the Church would be nice and tell lackeys like you the entire truth?! They're the ones who created this shitty Index system! Face the reality that's in front of you, and if you don't believe it, then just ask Index!!"

The two sorcerers, still dazed, looked at the girl standing behind the fissures.

"...No observable effect of Saint George's Hallowed Ground on intruder. Switching to alternate technique. Continuing attempt to destroy the intruder to safeguard the collar."

That was, without a doubt, the Index who the two sorcerers didn't know.

That was, without a doubt, the Index who the Church had kept hidden from them.

"..."

Enraged, Stiyl clamped his teeth together with enough force to crush them, but only for an instant.

"...Fortis931."

Thousands of cards flew out of the recesses of his black clothing.

The cards, each with a flame rune engraved on it, whipped into a whirlwind and completely plastered the floor, ceiling, and walls within moments. It was exactly like Hoichi the Earless, whose tattoos covered and protected his body.

But they weren't for Kamijou's benefit.

Stiyl placed his hand on Kamijou's back...so he could save Index.

"I don't need your vague possibilities. If we erase her memory, we can at least save her life **for now**. I'll kill anyone who gets between me and that goal. I will destroy whatever I have to! I made that decision long ago!"

Suddenly, Kamijou's legs, which had been steadily losing ground, stopped.

The tatami below him creaked under the unbelievable stress as he dug his toes in deeper.

"For...**now**?" He didn't turn back. "No, that's bullshit! That doesn't matter! I don't need logic or reasoning! Just answer me this, you sorcerer!!"

He drew in a breath.

"...Do you want to save Index?!"

The magician swallowed.

"You've both been waiting for this, haven't you? For a way you wouldn't have to take her memories—a way where you wouldn't have to be her enemies—the greatest and final happy ending where everybody gets to smile!"

His right wrist, straining under the pressure to keep the beam at bay, made a disturbing cracking noise.

But Kamijou still couldn't give up.

"This is the plot twist you've been waiting for! This isn't some filler dialogue that happens before the hero shows up! I'm not stalling for time before the main character appears! No one else, nothing else! Didn't you promise that you would save this girl with your own hands?!"

Bam! The nail of his right index finger splintered, and fresh crimson blood spurted through the fresh injuries.

But Kamijou still didn't want to give up.

"You've always wanted to be the main character! **You've always wanted to become the kind of sorcerer** you see in books and movies who risks his life to protect one girl! That's not over!! It hasn't even started!! Don't give up hope just because the prologue is a little long!!"

The sorcerer didn't respond.

Kamijou definitely wouldn't give up. What the sorcerers saw in him was anybody's guess.

"...If you just reach out, you can achieve it! Let's get this started already, sorcerers!"

A very nasty sound emanated from his right pinkie.

It bent at an unnatural angle...and broke. The instant this registered, the indescribably powerful pillar blew through his defense.

His right hand recoiled away.

The shaft of light rushed at his defenseless face at a speed beggaring imagination...

"...Salvare000!!"

Just before the pillar of light hit him, Kamijou heard Kanzaki shout.

It wasn't Japanese. It wasn't any language with which he was familiar. But he'd heard something similar—it was a name. It had been when he faced Stiyl in the student dormitory. It was the name Stiyl'd said all sorcerers must give when using sorcery—her magic name.

The katana Kanzaki held, close to two meters in length, sliced through the air. The Seven Glints, using the seven metal wires, approached Index with sound-splitting speed.

But her attack wasn't aimed at Index herself.

The seven metal wires shredded the frail tatami at Index's feet all at once. Suddenly without footing, she began falling backward. The magic circles linked to Index's eyes moved as well, causing the pillar of light aimed at Kamijou to miss its mark.

The beam swung upward like a giant sword, rending the wall, then the ceiling, leaving nothing in its wake. Even the black clouds floating in the night sky were torn open... It might even have sliced through satellites in low-Earth orbit.

Nothing remained of the portions of wall and ceiling the pillar had touched—not even a single splinter.

Instead, the eradicated sections turned into feathers of light, as pure and white as the beam itself. They were fluttering down. A few dozen of the feathers, effects unknown, danced through the summer night like snow.

"That's Dragon Breath... It's the same attack used by the legendary Saint George's Dragon! Whatever power you may possess, please don't consider letting it make contact with your body!"

Kamijou, who had escaped his battle with the light lance, listened to Kanzaki as he shot toward Index, now crumpled on the floor.

Before he could reach her, though, Index's head moved.

The pillar of light that had torn a hole through the night sky started to swing back down.

It'll catch me again!

"... Innocentius!"

As Kamijou prepared himself for the blow, a whirlpool of flame materialized before him.

The giant fire took on human form and spread its arms to stand as a shield to block the light.

It looked like a cross protecting someone from sin.

"Go, esper!" He heard Stiyl's voice. "Her time limit's already passed! If you're going to try something, then don't waste a second!!"

Kamijou didn't answer. Neither did he look back.

Instead, he ran toward Index, detouring around the clashing flame and light—because Stiyl wanted him to. Kamijou had heard his words, knew what he meant by them, and understood all the feelings they implied.

Kamijou ran.

Ran!!

"...Warning. Reading from chapter six, verse thirteen. New enemies confirmed. Modifying combat processes. Beginning battlefield scan...Complete. Prioritizing the destruction of the most immediately dangerous enemy soldier, Touma Kamijou."

Index's head came down, and the pillar of light followed with a loud blast.

However, at the same time, the Witch-Hunter King moved in to block for Kamijou. The light and flame ate into each other, each repeating the cycle of destruction and rebirth.

Kamijou ran straight for Index, now defenseless.

Four more meters.

Three more meters.

Two more meters!

One more meter!!

"Wait, stop! Above you!!" Kanzaki's voice rang out, cutting through the chaos, just as Kamijou was about to reach out and touch the magic circles in front of Index. He looked at the ceiling without cutting his stride.

The feathers of light.

Dozens of shining, glittering feathers created when Index's beam destroyed the wall and ceiling. They drifted down through the air like snowflakes and were about to alight on his head.

Kamijou didn't know much about magic, but he got the picture. If even one of those things was to touch him, he'd be in big trouble.

He also knew that if he used his right hand, they could easily be canceled out.

However…

"…Warning. Reading from chapter twenty-two, verse one. Flame magic technique successfully reverse engineered. Distorted cross image confirmed to be created by runes. Building technique for anti-cross use…Type One, Type Two, Type Three. Twenty seconds until complete activation of Eri Eri Rema Sabaktani."

The color of the pillar of light started to change from pure white to a bloody crimson.

Innocentius's revival speed began to wane, and it started to be pushed toward the light.

Dealing with the dozens of glowing feathers with his right hand one at a time would probably take too long. Index could regain her posture, and Kamijou knew that the Witch-Hunter King wouldn't last much longer.

Above him were dozens of dancing wings of illumination.

At his feet was a lone girl whose feelings were being abused and whose body was being manipulated like a puppet.

The only question was which one he would save. The other would fall. It was simple.

Of course, the answer was already decided.

Touma Kamijou hadn't been using his right hand to protect himself during these battles.

He'd been fighting the sorcerers all along to protect this one girl.

All right, God, if the story of this world really does follow your system…

He opened the five fingers of his right fist.

He stretched them out straight, as if about to strike with his palm.

…Then I'll bust up that illusion first!!

And then, he brought down his right hand.

The black fissures and the magic circles creating them.

Kamijou's right hand cleanly sliced through them all.

It severed them so easily that he wanted to laugh at how much he'd endured just to get this far.

It cut them effortlessly, as if they were no sturdier than the paper nets used to catch goldfish at festivals.

"...War...ning. Reading from...final...chapter, verse...zero... Collar has...sustained critical...regeneration...impossible...era—"

Suddenly, Index's voice completely disappeared.

The pillar of light disappeared as well, as did the magic circles, and the fissures running throughout the room began to retract as if being rubbed out with a pencil eraser...

At that moment, one of the light feathers landed on Kamijou's head.

He thought for a moment he heard someone shouting.

He didn't know whether it was Stiyl, or Kanzaki, or even himself, or maybe Index. Maybe she had woken up.

His entire body, all the way down to his fingertips, was sapped of its strength from that one hit, as if he had been smashed in the head with a metal hammer.

Kamijou collapsed on top of Index, who was herself still huddled on the floor...

...As if to cover her from the glowing feathers raining down upon them.

Just like snow piling up, dozens of illuminated feathers danced down to blanket Kamijou's body.

Touma Kamijou was still laughing.

While he laughed, his fingers ceased moving permanently.

That night...

...Touma Kamijou died.

FINAL CHAPTER

The Forbidden Book Girl's Conclusion
Index Librorum Prohibitorum.

"Miss, you don't have any, do you?"

The plump doctor posed his question in the examination room of a university hospital.

Spinning around on his revolving chair, the doctor wore a small tree-frog sticker on the ID card on his chest, perhaps because he knew he looked like a frog.

Index was a philanthropist, but scientists were an exception. She didn't like them.

It was true that sorcerers were a bunch of weirdos, but she considered scientists to be even worse.

She wanted to complain about being alone with a person like this, but as she didn't have anyone with her, she couldn't.

She was alone.

"I think it's a bit strange to speak so formally with someone who isn't even a patient, so I'll stop, okay? This is my first and last question to you as a doctor: Why exactly did you come to the hospital?"

Index didn't know herself.

No one—not a single person—had told her what really happened.

The sorcerers, who she'd thought were her enemies, had told her they had been erasing her memories annually up until now, and that a single young man had risked his life to save her from that accursed cycle, but she didn't understand it.

"But oh my, there were three people running around in Academy City without identification? One of the observation satellites got shot out of the sky by a mysterious flash; I bet Judgment is all over the place now."

That was more than one question, thought Index.

Three people without IDs... She was one of them, so the other two were probably the sorcerers. They had just delivered Index to the hospital and left, despite having chased her around for so long.

"By the way, **they** gave you that letter in your hands, right?"

The frog-faced doctor looked at the envelope Index carried. It looked like a love letter.

Index got irritated, ripped open the envelope, and removed its contents.

"Whoa! I think that was meant for the young man, not you..."

"It's fine," answered Index, annoyed.

The letter was suspicious in the first place. The sender was labeled as "Stiyl Magnus," and it was addressed "Dear Touma Kamijou." She detected a murderous malice in the heart-shaped sticker on the envelope.

There's no point in formalities, so I'll make this brief.

I'd love to say I'm amazed that you actually did it, you asshole, but if I were going to write to you about that, I could cut down every tree in the world and still need more paper, so I won't do that, dick.

There were eight sheets of stationery in the same vein. Index wordlessly crumpled each one into a neat ball and tossed it over her shoulder. The frog doctor's face became steadily and increasingly flustered as she cluttered up his work area, but he was unable to say anything to Index, as she exhibited the air of a bullied child on the verge of tears.

Finally, on the ninth page, the last, the following was written:

In any case, as the bare minimum of gratitude I owe you for ***helping us out****, I'll explain about the girl and her circumstances, since I don't want you coming around and asking for favors in the future. We'll definitely be enemies the next time we meet, I've decided.*

We were still uneasy leaving her with you scientists, so while the doctor was away, we sorcerers checked up on Index, but she seems fine. The order handed down from the English Puritan Church is, on its face, to bring her back as soon as possible, since her 'collar' was taken off, but in reality, it's closer to just telling us to keep an eye on her. Though, personally, I cringe at the thought of leaving her at your side for one more second.

She was able to use the 103,000 grimoires for magic even though the Church set up John's Pen inside her. And now that John's Pen itself has been destroyed, we don't know whether she can use magic of her own volition. If, hypothetically, her magical power was replenished when she lost John's Pen, then we're going to have to make preparations for that as well.

Well, I don't really think magical power can be recovered just like that. But you can never be too careful, I guess. A demon god that could use all 103,000 grimoires would be just that dangerous.

(Incidentally, this doesn't mean I'm giving up and handing her over to you, got it? After we've prepared and acquired enough information, we plan on challenging you and taking her back again. I'm not a fan of killing people in their sleep, so keep an eye peeled for us, or you'll regret it.)

P.S. I booby-trapped this letter to explode when you finish reading it. Although you may have found out the truth, it's your punishment for that selfish gamble, so I hope it at least blows a finger off of that right hand you're so proud of.

Immediately below that, at the end of the letter, one of Stiyl's runes had been inscribed.

As she panicked and threw the letter from her hands, it burst into little pieces with a crackling sound.

"Your friends are pretty violent, aren't they? I wonder if they painted it with a liquid explosive or something."

He was completely unsurprised. She seriously almost thought he was crazy.

But maybe because Index was so emotionally numb, she was incapable of articulating a more complex thought.

So she'd just fulfilled the mission she'd come to the hospital to perform.

"If you're wondering about the young man, it'd probably be quicker to go see for yourself."

The frog-faced doctor seemed very amused.

"Looking shocked in front of him would be rude, though, so I'll give you a few quick tips before you go in."

She knocked on the door to the hospital room twice.

That alone made Index's heart feel as if it might burst. While waiting for a reply, she fidgeted, wiped the sweat on her palms onto the hem of her habit to dry them, and then crossed herself.

"Yes?" came the voice of a young man.

Index grabbed the handle, wondering if she should ask if it was okay to come in. But she was scared of him calling her annoying and to come in already. Very, very scared.

She opened the door with all the grace of a stilted robot. It wasn't a shared six-person ward, but rather a personal room for a single patient. Perhaps because the walls, floor, and ceiling were all completely white, it threw off her sense of distance and made it feel more expansive than it actually was.

The young man was sitting up on the antiseptically white bed.

The window next to the bed was open, and the bleached curtains were billowing into the room.

He was alive.

That fact in and of itself almost brought Index to tears. She wondered if she should leap onto him and hug him now or bite his head first for acting so recklessly.

"Excuse me...," he began. His head was wrapped in bandages like headbands. He tilted it in puzzlement.

"I think you may have the wrong room."

The young man's words carried a very polite tone, but they were mingled with a little bit of suspicion as he tried to figure out what was going on.

It was a voice normally reserved for a stranger over the phone.

"...It's not really amnesia, but rather 'memory destruction.'"

The words the doctor had imparted in an icy examination room shielded from the summer heat resurfaced in the back of Index's mind.

"...It's not that he lost his memories, but that those brain cells were destroyed. I don't think he'll ever remember anything. Did you guys open him up and zap his spine with a Taser or what?"

"...Nh."

Index stopped breathing and let her gaze fall to the floor helplessly.

The boy's brain had been gravely damaged as a side effect of both forcing himself to use his power for too long and the pillar of light that she herself had apparently shot at him. (She didn't actually remember anything.)

If that was just a physical thing... a "wound," then they might have been able to do something with a healing spell, like when Index had been slashed in the back. However, the transparent youth had a right hand called Imagine Breaker. Regardless of the intentions, good or evil, it would dispel magic of any kind.

In other words, even if they tried to mend him, the healing magic itself would be nullified.

The simple fact of the matter was that this poor soul had died on the inside rather than the outside.

"Excuse me...?" came his uneasy—or rather, concerned—voice.

For some reason, Index couldn't forgive the voice that was coming out of the hollow boy.

He had been injured for her sake, but he was worried about her. That just wasn't fair.

Index took a deep breath, as if swallowing whatever it was rising in her chest.

She thought she could probably manage a smile.

Her friend was completely empty, and he didn't remember anything at all about Index.

"Excuse me, are you all right? You look like you're in a lot of pain."

Unfortunately, her perfectly constructed smile was shattered with one blow. Thinking back, she remembered he had always tried to see the true feelings that she kept hidden behind her smile.

"No, I'm okay," Index said, exhaling. "Of course I'm okay."

The transparent young man studied Index's face for a little while.

"... Excuse me, could it be that we know each other?"

That question, above all the others, hit Index the hardest.

Because it was proof that the transparent boy didn't know anything about her.

Not a thing. Not a single thing.

"Yeah...," she answered, standing alone in the middle of the room, looking every bit like an elementary schooler being punished for forgetting her homework.

"Touma, don't you remember? When we met on the balcony in your dormitory?"

"... I lived in a dorm, huh?"

"... Touma, don't you remember? When you destroyed my Walking Church with your right hand?"

"... What's a Walking Church? A church of people who walk a lot?"

"...... Touma, don't you remember? When you fought the sorcerers to protect me?"

"... Whose name is Touma?"

Her mouth was about to stop moving.

"Touma, you don't remember?"

But she wanted to ask him this one thing.

"How much Index loved you?"

"I'm sorry," said the boy, without any feeling behind his words.

"Who's Index? It's not a person's name. Did I have a dog or a cat or something?"

The shock struck her hard, and a fierce urge to cry swelled in her chest.

But Index swallowed it, trying to force all that down.

Burying it inside her, she smiled. It was far from a perfect smile—it was probably very ragged at best.

* * *

"Oh, man, I really got you! Aha-ha-ha!!"

"Huh... ?" Index froze.

The hollow boy's anxiousness had disappeared. In its place was a widening, ferociously savage, wicked grin. His canines were showing. It was as if he'd been swapped with someone else.

"What are you getting so worked up about being called a pet? Are you one of those people who's *into* collars? I'll tell you what, I've got no intention of going for the 'interested in jailbait' ending here."

Color had returned to the transparent youth's face while she wasn't looking.

Index didn't understand what was going on. She rubbed her eyes hard to make sure she wasn't hallucinating and dug around in her ear with a finger to make sure she wasn't hearing things. It felt as if one shoulder of her perfectly fitted habit had started sliding down.

"What? Huh? Touma? What? But he said you forgot everything 'cause your brain got blown up..."

"...Hey, why are you acting like you *wanted* me to forget?" Kamijou sighed. "You're such a dullard. Yeah, at the very end, I decided to let all those light feather things come down on me. I have no idea what they were supposed to do, since I'm not a sorcerer or anything, but from what the doctor told me, they injured my brain cells. And that I should have lost my memories because of it, or something?"

"Should have?"

"Yep. I mean, wasn't the damage just another magical power?"

"Ah." Index gasped.

"That's how it is. That's how it went; that's how it'll be. No matter how you put it, it's simple—if I put my hand on my head and use the Imagine Breaker on myself, then problem solved."

"Ah." Index exhaled, then sunk to the floor.

"Basically, before the damage can get from my body to my brain, I can just cancel out the magical injuries. Well, if it had been a physical phenomenon like Stiyl's flames, it wouldn't have worked, but those feathers of light were just some weird abnormal power, so there was no problem."

Like cutting the fuse before the flame could ignite the bomb, he'd canceled the shock before the damage afflicted the brain.

It was ridiculous.

It was ridiculous, but when Index thought about it, the Imagine Breaker could even dispel miracles—God's own rules.

She was dazed. Just dazed. Index, having fallen to her knees, dumbstruck, looked up at Kamijou. She could now honestly declare that the shoulder of her habit had come loose, and the confusion on her face confirmed it.

"Pfft! You should have seen your face! You're always volunteering to sacrifice yourself. Maybe after what happened, you'll look at your behavior differently?"

"..." Index didn't answer.

"...Er, huh?...Um, excuse me..."

Even Kamijou was forced to lower his tone awkwardly at her silence.

Her face slowly slid down, and her long silver hair obscured her expression.

Her shoulders shook as she sat there. She didn't know why, but she gritted her teeth.

In an infinitely unpleasant tone, Kamijou couldn't help but ask.

"Umm, might I venture a question, princess?"

"What is it?" Index answered.

"Are, uh, you...actually, er, mad?"

The patient's call button rang.

The screams of a boy being bitten on the head reverberated throughout the hospital ward.

Index stormed out of the patient's room, uttering pouty noises as she left.

"Whoops." Kamijou heard a voice outside the doorway. It seemed the frog-faced doctor had almost run into Index as they were trading places.

"There was a nurse call, but... Ah, this is terrible."

The upper half of the young man's body was slipping off the bed, and he was cradling the top of his head with both hands and crying. It was, strangely, realistically scary; he kept mumbling to himself, "I'm gonna die; I'm really gonna die."

The doctor looked at the opened door one more time, returning his gaze to the hospital room and Kamijou.

"Was that okay with you?"

"What?" the young man answered.

"You don't actually remember anything, do you?"

The transparent boy was silent.

The reality ordained by God was neither as warm nor as fuzzy as the story he'd fed to the girl.

The student, who had been incapacitated due to a brush with some magic, had been transported to the hospital with Index by a man and a woman calling themselves sorcerers. They had told the doctor everything that had transpired. The doctor didn't believe any of it, of course, but respecting his patient's rights, relayed the information to the young man as it had been explained.

Listening to the story had been no different than reading from someone else's diary.

He didn't know what the girl in the diary—whose face he could not place with the unfamiliar name—had done.

After all, the story now was nothing more than a fiction written based on a third person's journal.

Even though he was told that his bandage-covered right hand possessed the power to kill miracles, God's own rules...

...there was no way he could bring himself to believe it.

"But I think this is fine," the transparent young man told the doctor.

Even though it was just someone else's diary, it was still fun and painful.

Even though his memories would never come back…

He somehow got the impression that it was a very sad situation.

"I don't know why, but I felt like she's somebody I'd never want to see cry. I could put together at least that much. I don't know how to describe the emotion, and I probably won't ever remember it, but that's definitely how I felt."

The transparent boy smiled, but it was once more devoid of color.

"But Doctor, why'd you buy a story like that? Sorcerers and magic—aren't they the polar opposite of the world you live in?"

"Not at all," the frog-faced doctor answered proudly. "Hospitals and the occult are pretty closely linked, you know?…I don't mean that ghosts show up in hospitals or anything. But we have to deal with churches saying no transfusions, no surgery, and bringing lawsuits against us even if we save someone's life, you know. For a doctor, 'occult' just means to 'do as the patient says for now.'"

The doctor smiled.

He didn't know why he was smiling, but when he looked at the young patient's grin, he felt like smiling, too, like a mirror.

But which one of them was the mirror?

There was nothing behind the boy's smile. He couldn't even detect any sadness.

The young man was just absolutely blank.

"Strangely enough, I might actually still remember."

The frog-faced doctor looked at his transparent patient, a bit surprised.

"Your memories died along with your brain cells, though?"

That was a lame thing to say, even for me, thought the doctor immediately after saying it.

But he went on to ask the following anyway:

"It's like a computer hard drive being burned to a crisp. If there's no information left in your brain, then where would you say those memories could possibly come from?"

He asked it because for some reason…

…he thought that the boy would somehow dispel the logic for him.

"Where? That's obvious," the transparent boy answered.

"My soul, right?"

AFTERWORD

Pleased to meet you. I'm Kazuma Kamachi.

I feel fiercely embarrassed about introducing myself using my pen name. Think about the first time you told people your Internet username, and you get the idea.

Speaking of the Internet, that's where the opportunity to write this book originated.

RPGs and the like have these magicians that can use MP to do anything from shooting fireballs to resurrecting the dead. They can do anything. It's really convenient. But I thought: Well, what sort of people were the magicians who actually existed throughout history (or at least are said to have existed)? Everyone uses the term *magic*, but what kind of logic did that magic follow? I figured I'd clear up these questions, so I went on a search engine and typed in words like *sorcerer* and *real* to investigate. That's where it all started.

What I got back were things like "how to control black cats using silver vine powder," "voodoo shamans using the poison of a puffer fish to create a temporarily dead zombie," and I was like, *What?* For occult stuff, this is all pretty scientific, isn't it? That's how I formed an interest.

Many Dengeki Bunko light novels use magic in them as if it's an everyday occurrence, so I started thinking that a work that delved more deeply into the inner workings would be new and fresh.

...Well, this book is just basically entirely what I felt like writing, completely disregarding "marketing studies investigating reader thoughts (read: catchy themes)." I cannot be thankful enough for my editor, Ms. Miki, and my illustrator, Kiyotaka Haimura. Thank you both so much.

And a huge "thank-you" to the readers, the ones who picked up this book and read the whole, long thing straight through to the end.

As I hope that the Touma Kamijou and Index in your hearts can live on a little longer,

and as I pray that I can write a second volume,

today, at this moment, I lay down my pen.

....................................It's actually still December 26, 2003.

Kazuma Kamachi